WET DREAMS ON LOCKDOWN

The Nurse

ELIJAH R. FREEMAN

URBAN AINT DEAD

URBAN AINT DEAD
P.O Box 448
Maybrook, NY 12543

Cover Design: P. Wise / The Wise Services

Contact Author on FB: Elijah R. Freeman / IG: @the_future_of_urban_fiction

Contact Publisher at www.urbanaintdead.com

Email: urbanaintdead@gmail.com

ISBN: 979-8-9902387-0-1

CONTENTS

———————————

SOUNDTRACKS

———————————

Scan the QR Code below to listen to the Soundtracks/Singles of some of your favorite U.A.D titles:

Don't have Spotify or Apple Music?
No Sweat!
Visit your choice streaming platform and search URBAN AINT DEAD.

Currently on lock serving a bid?
JPay, iHeartRadio, WHATEVER!
We got you covered.

Simply log into your facility's kiosk or tablet, go to music and
search URBAN AINT DEAD.

SUBMISSIONS

Submit the first three chapters of your completed manuscript to urbanaintdead@gmail.com, subject line: Your book's title. The manuscript must be in a .doc file and sent as an attachment. The document should be in Times New Roman, double-spaced, and in size 12 font. Also, provide your synopsis and full contact information. If sending multiple submissions, they must each be in a separate email. Have a story but no way to submit it electronically? You can still submit to URBAN AINT DEAD. Send in the first three chapters, written or typed, of your completed manuscript to:

URBAN AINT DEAD
P.O Box 448
Maybrook, NY 12543

DO NOT send original manuscript. Must be a duplicate.
Provide your synopsis and a cover letter containing your full contact information.
Thanks for considering URBAN AINT DEAD.

Chapter 1

"Ow! Goddamn, bitch! Why you squeezing it so hard? That shit hurts!"

Dominique sighed as she squeezed the inmate's eyebrows together to stop the bleeding. The prison nurse was frustrated with the inmate that she was helping.

He was a scrawny, black male who she was sure was on drugs, tweaking out. Somehow, he had gotten his eyebrow slit open and she needed to get the bleeding under control so she could see if he would need stitches or not.

"I'm sorry, Mr. Kemp, but I have to get this bleeding under control so I can determine how deep it is. I know it doesn't feel good, but I need you to bear with me. I'll be able to get you some pain meds after."

"Pain meds? What kind of meds?"

Dominique had to resist the urge to roll her eyes when he perked up at the mention of pain meds. His reaction had confirmed her suspicions. He was a drug addict looking for a fix, which was more than likely the reason he ended up in the nurses' office in the first place.

"Tylenol. Now sit still, please," she said dismissively.

The man mumbled something under his breath but sat still. Every once in a while, he would wince when she applied pressure to his brow, to see if the bleeding had stopped.

Dominique held her breath, only breathing through her mouth while she patched the man up because the stench that rolled off of him was so foul, that she struggled not to gag. Further validating her thoughts that his visit to her was drug-related. It was common for inmates to sell their hygiene products and rarely shower.

Ten minutes later, she applied petroleum jelly to his brow and put a Band-Aid over it. "Alright, Mr. Kemp. You're all patched up." Turning around, she walked over to a cupboard, grabbed a bottle of Tylenol and a small plastic cup, dropped two tablets into it, then handed it to him. "Take these, and the guard will go ahead and escort you back to your dorm."

"Thank you, beautiful." The inmate said as he hopped off of the medical table.

Dominique knocked on the office door and it opened up right away. The C.O. standing on the other side gestured for the man to come out.

Dominique didn't respond to the man as he walked out of

the room. Once the officer that was standing outside of the door closed it behind them, she rolled her eyes. Getting called things like "beautiful," "sexy," and "gorgeous" after being cussed out for attempting to help the injured or sickly inmates wasn't anything new. She was used to it for the most part. None of the compliments that she got from any of them flattered her. She always assumed that it was just jail talk, anyway. Many of the inmates had been locked up for long periods of time, so naturally, most of them that came to her office were able to appreciate her natural beauty.

Dominique was a full-figured, five-foot-seven. The middle part of her name had earned her the nickname, Mini, but she was far from that. A plus-size woman, she had ample breast, thick thighs and a nice, plump ass, something she couldn't hide under her scrubs. Her mahogany skin was flawless, showing that she took good care of herself and had a high water intake. She had a pretty face, free of any traces of make-up, allowing her natural beauty to shine through daily.

The sound of a familiar and rhythmic knock at the door, caught her attention. "Come in!" She ripped off the disposable paper on the medical table, in preparation for the next patient. Grabbing a can of Lysol, she sprayed and wiped the faux leather material down before covering it with more paper.

"You good, girl?" Her best friend and co-worker Sierra asked as walked in. Sierra was a Correctional Officer there at Valdosta State Prison. The two had been childhood best friends and they loved being able to work together.

"Yeah, why you ask that?" Dominique turned around to look at her friend. The worry that she heard in her voice threw her for a loop.

"I was just making sure. That nigga that just left outta here is a weirdo. Got his head busted 'cause he don't pay his debts. I just got done talkin' to my lil boo and he let me know what was going on. I just wanted to check on you and make sure that junkie wasn't bothering you. I'll have his ass jumped on again if he tried you." Sierra pulled the large band holding her braids together in a bun, letting them cascade down her back.

Dominique gave her friend a disapproving look. "Well, I'm fine, so don't feel the need to have nobody jumped on my behalf." She shook her head as she went to a cupboard and used a set of keys to unlock it so she could access the supply of hypodermic needles and insulin. The next inmate that was due to see her was a diabetic that would need his insulin shot. "I see you still fuckin' around with these inmates. You ain't learn yo lesson last time?"

Sierra rolled her eyes at Dominique's concern as she worked to put her braids back in a bun. They had been too tight and were giving her a headache. With six hours left on her shift, the relief was much needed. "You so boring. Instead of worrying about me, *you* should have a little fun and find one of these niggas to fuck wit', too. Some of these niggas in here got long dick *and* money. Make this shit work for you, girl! You workin' *two* jobs when you could just work here and get in good with one of these bosses in here."

Once Sierra was done re-doing her hair, she put her hands on her hips and watched Dominique maneuver around the room. After preparing the necessary supplies that she would need to tend to her next patient, she sat at the computer to document what she had done for Mr. Kemp. Documentation was necessary. If there was no record, it didn't happen. Each inmate was required to pay a five-dollar co-pay fee whenever they visited medical, and the medical supervisor did not play about them co-pays. Dominique didn't have the time or patience for a lecture

"I don't know. I've thought about it, but I don't wanna lose my license. I worked too hard and am in too much debt to risk it messing around with a criminal." She said as she began typing on the computer.

"There you go being judgmental and shit. Just 'cause niggas are criminals and in prison doesn't mean they're bad people. I mean, shit, you know that *I* do what I do 'cause I have to. I have kids to feed, and I don't have time to go out and date because I work so much. This is all convenient for me. It could be convenient for you, too. Hell, you *need* some dick. Maybe then you wouldn't be so uptight."

Sierra had been urging her friend to "have fun" with some of the inmates while making some extra cash in the process for the last three months. The idea had never been something that settled right with Dominique, but at times she did feel tempted. Of the two friends, she was the good girl, always aiming to do the right thing and remain on the right side of the law.

But Dominique's thoughts often wandered into the forbidden territory that Sierra so casually inhabited. She could almost taste the thrill of the unknown, the allure of quick money, and the rush of stepping outside her own meticulously drawn lines. Every time Sierra shared her tales of excitement and gain, something in Dominique's chest tightened—a mix of fear, lust, and curiosity.

At night, alone with her thoughts, Dominique would sometimes catch herself crafting scenarios in her mind where she crossed that invisible line, just to feel the adrenaline of the *what if*. She had even strummed her clit a few times to prison nurse porn. Yet she clung to her principles like a life raft, reminding herself of the consequences, the betrayal of her values, and the disappointment of those she loved.

Even when Sierra pointed out the seemingly harmless nature of it all, or how easy it was, Dominique found herself wet with need, her face a well-rehearsed mask hiding her internal conflict. She was teetering on a precipice, drawn by the siren call of temptation, yet every time she peered over the edge, her heart recoiled, and she stepped back, reaffirming her resolve.

The truth was, Dominique wanted to try it, to break free from her restraints, if only for a moment, but she couldn't—wouldn't—admit it.

So she remained the good girl, the anchor in the storm of

Sierra's schemes, quietly patching the cracks in her armor and hoping that, with time, the temptation would fade into a distant memory, never to be realized. Dominique understood the stakes were high, and the cost of losing herself in the depths of that enticing darkness was far too great. There was, after all, no turning back from some choices, and she wasn't willing to gamble with the life she had so carefully built.

"Are you done?" Dominique asked, typing away at the computer.

"Fuck you, bitch. Fine... one day yo ass gonna see what I'm talking about. All it's gonna take is the right nigga to walk in this office and it'll be a wrap. Watch."

Dominique looked over her shoulder to see Sierra's tall, slim-petite frame halfway out of the door. The woman pointed a short, baby pink painted acrylic nail at her, her pretty chocolate skin seemingly glowing from within. "I'ma getchu." Then she slipped fully out of the door, the heavy metal shutting hard behind her.

Dominique rolled her eyes, let out a heavy sigh, and shook her head before returning to the task of documenting her last visit.

A part of her was frustrated. She was extremely tired and in the middle of a twenty-four-hour shift. After completing a grueling twelve-hour shift at South Georgia Medical Center, she headed directly to the prison to endure another eight-hour stint. Once her duties there concluded, she would be granted a mere two hours of rest before returning to the hospital for an additional four hours of work. To say she was exhausted would be an understatement.

As she worked, her best friend's words were repeating over and over in her head. It was true that she worked so long and hard that she barely even had time for herself, let alone a man. She often felt lonely, intimacy and affection being things that she craved but was virtually impossible thanks to the fact that she had to work so much. While Sierra hadn't been wrong, the risk seemed far greater than the reward.

Plus, there hadn't been one inmate that came into her office that she had been even slightly attracted to. None of them were her type and none of them she found worthy of giving her pussy up to.

Fucking with an inmate at Valdosta State Prison was out.

"AIN'T NO MUFUCKIN' way, bruh. I know I'm not trippin'! My shit was in my box and now it's not. Where the fuck is my shit?"

Ramello shook his head as he sat on his cot, texting on his cell phone. Nine other Muslims were present in the cell as well, posted up arms folded or standing about except for Badazz, who was tweaking out because his phone and some of his work had gone missing from his locker box. Around him in the tight space of Ramello's cell, the Muslims had gathered to figure out what was going on.

Earlier, Badazz had rushed out of his cell to catch a play at the door and threw his stuff on the bottom shelf under some clothes. On his way back, he was stopped by someone on the wall phone who needed his Cash App while he had his people on the line. The dorm officer, who he was cool with, called his name to help grab the ice cooler for the dorm at the front gate, so he assisted and now his property was missing.

Ramello looked up to see the man's anger written all over his face. The vein in his neck stood out, thick and prominent, as he yelled, his fist slamming into his hand as he spoke each word.

"My shit ain't up and walk away by itself, bruh. Somebody in this mufucka got my shit and if it doesn't come up, I'm finna flip this bitch! I don't give a fuck if I gotta free-pick a nigga!"

Ramello scratched at the stubble of his beard and looked around the room, gauging the reaction of the eight other Muslims squeezed into his cell. It was clear that a thief was among them and needed to be weeded out.

"As-salamu-Alakum, Ahki. Calm down. We gon' figure this shit out." Jihad, an OG attempted to soothe the young hothead. "Look, they about to call Chow. Y'all all go and while y'all out, I'ma go see if anybody seen anything. Aiight?"

The older man looked young for his age, having taken good care of his body by being disciplined in his eating and workout habits. He was a level-headed man that who kept their operations running smoothly and was well respected and known to be extremely deadly. A lifer with no chance of parole, he took his job seriously. It gave him purpose.

"Nah, fuck that–"

"Come on, bruh, we ain't even about to be down there that long. Let him do what he gotta do so we can get yo shit back." Fetty, another Muslim, and one of Badazz's closest friends put a hand on his shoulder and began pushing him toward the door.

As if on cue, chow was being called.

Badazz was going to protest but stopped as the rest of his brothers began filing out of the room. He released a frustrated sigh and followed behind them.

Ramello and his bunkmate Haniyf were the only two that remained.

"Who you think did it? A lot of shit been coming up missin' lately..." Haniyf cleared his things from his bed and began putting them in one of the spots that he had a junkie build in the wall of his cell.

"Ain't no tellin'. I wish a nigga would try that shit wit' me, though. Get his ass fucked over." Ramello grabbed his knife from under his pillow and tucked it into his waistline. "You goin' to chow?"

"Hell yea, Bro. I'm hungry as a mufucka." Haniyf began sealing the spot.

"Hold up, then, nigga. If yeen goin', I need to put my shit up, too." Ramello handed Haniyf his phone, they sealed it in the spot and together they made their way to the chow hall.

Twenty minutes later, Ramello and Haniyf were walking back to their cell when they noticed that the door was slightly ajar. "The fuck?" Ramello said and snatched the door open to find a short, dirty, lanky nigga named Bart bent over searching under his mat. He looked up, and his eyes widened with fear.

"Melly!"

"The fuck!?

"Wazzam, nephew? I was just—" his eyes darted wildly around the room until they landed back on his mat. "Fixin' ya bed. Yea, fixin' ya bed for you." He reached for the covers and Ramello rushed him.

"Arggg!" Bart yelled in pain, and charged at Ramello headfirst in an attempt to defend himself.

The only thing that could be heard was the scuffling of shoes and banging against walls, bed and locker box.

"Yeah, fuck that nigga up, Melly!" Haniyf shouted as he egged Ramello on.

Ramello was in a rage, almost in disbelief that a nigga had the nerve to think it was sweet for him to come in his shit and even *attempt* to take some shit from him. The fact that he had caught him in the act only pissed him off even further. His six-foot-two frame towered over the much shorter man as he let off a barrage of punches all over the man's body.

"Oh, shit! Melly! Mell! Mell, man stop!" Ramello heard Jihad and the concerned voices of others. The urgency in their tones was muffled by the beat of his fury, causing him to barely register their presence as they rushed to see what the commotion was about.

It wasn't until two of his brothers were pulling him off of the thief that he let up. "Yeah, fuck nigga! Thought you could try that shit wit' me. I'm on yo ass every mufuckin' time I see you."

"Chill, nigga, look at yo leg! We gotta get'chu to medical. We gon' take care of him. You gotta go." Worry was evident in Jihad's voice as he tried to calm Ramello down.

Badazz stabbed Bart in the head, sending blood splattering on the wall. Fetty, Haniyf, and five more Muslims began stomping and kicking him as he balled up and screamed.

Ramello was so worked up that he hadn't noticed the big red stain on his thigh that was growing and spreading down his pants leg. It seemed as if the moment he laid eyes on the blood seeping through his white pants, a sharp pain began to shoot through his thigh.

"Man, what the fuck?!" He pulled at the large slit that went almost entirely across the width of his thigh. Pieces of pink and brown flesh peeked through the slit in his pants as blood spewed from the wound heavily. "This nigga stabbed me?" He was in disbelief.

"Officer! We need medical!" Jihad was at the dorm's door, banging on it repeatedly attempting to get the attention of the officer sitting in the booth.

Moments later, Sierra was popping the door and stepping

in to see what the issue was. Her eyes widened the moment she laid eyes on Ramello and saw the large blood stain and rip in his pants. With a guy at each side of him, helping him walk, he limped towards her.

"Ms. Jones! Ms. Jones! We got one need to go to medical," one of the guys said.

Someone getting stabbed at a level 5 prison was normal, and usually wouldn't have been taken as seriously but an inmate had just died the week before due to a leg wound. He had only been stabbed once but that was all it took when you hit a major artery.

"Come on! Come on! Come on!" She frantically waved him over as she held the door open, her eyes quickly scanning the dorm looking for signs of any distress. Besides a few stray people sitting around at tables or poking their heads out of the door, she didn't notice anything out of the norm. Nothing stuck out to her immediately, so she decided not to call a code until she could figure out what was going on. She had just dropped off a pack to her boo and didn't want to make the dorm hot if she could avoid it. "Shit! Does anybody else need medical attention?" She asked skeptically as Ramello slipped past her into the sallyport.

"Nah, just him," Jihad said.

Sierra closed the door, locking it instantly. Ramello squinted his eyes from the sunlight and watched as Sierra popped the sallyport gate. He walked out and she escorted him to Medical, glad the walk was deserted besides all the pollen that stained the ground. Their dorm had been the last dorm to get fed lunch and administration had cleared the walk afterwards. "You wanna tell me what happened? Do I need to call a code, sir?" Sierra asked as she knocked on the Medical door.

"Nah, I'm straight. I cut myself on accident." Ramello took a deep breath. The pain in his leg was beginning to get to him. The feeling of the thick and sticky blood and the burning sensation from being cut seemed to be getting more intense the longer that it was exposed to air, and the more he walked. He was gripping his leg, applying pressure at the top to slow the bleeding.

They watched through the glass as Dominique approached, and when she snatched the door open Sierra made a noise, but said nothing. Dominique's eyes widened for a moment before she stepped forward to grab Ramello by the arm and help him into a backroom.

"Oh my, help me get him on the table." Dominique ushered him over to the medical table.

Closing the door, Sierra and Dominique carefully helped Ramello lie on the medical table. "Hand me those scissors over there," Dominique pointed to a pair that was on the table behind her. "What's your name, sir?"

"Dixon..." Ramello seemed calm as he lay on the table. He was in pain and in slight disbelief as he processed what happened to him. He didn't know how he got stabbed. He hadn't even expected the dirty nigga to have been strapped, but it had happened nevertheless. He wished he had known that he was hit before he was pulled off of him or he would have fucked the nigga up even more. He was thankful that he hadn't because he probably would have killed the nigga.

"Hi, Dixon. I'm Nurse Dominique. I'm gonna have to cut these pants off of you, okay?" Her voice was calm and soft as she spoke.

Ramello looked up and met the prettiest, brown, almond-shaped eyes. He couldn't remember the last time that he had been in such close proximity to a woman. Seven years, he had been behind the wall, and three years had gone by since he had a visit from a woman as well. The nurse's kind eyes were unexpectedly comforting to him. "Aiight..." He said and watched as the pretty woman took the scissors from Sierra and began to cut from the bottom of his left pants leg, all the way up to the waistband, and then flipped the material open so she could free his leg.

Cling!

"Oop!" they all looked at the floor to see Ramello's knife had fallen from his waistline.

"I'll get that." Sierra squatted, picked it up, and put it in her pocket.

Dominique shook it off and focused her attention back on his leg.

"Goddamn!" Sierra gasped when she saw the large gash, seeping blood.

Dominique looked back at her friend and gave her a nasty look.

"My bad." She threw her hands up.

"Go grab him a cup of water." The nurse said as she shook her head.

Ramello got a good look at her when she turned around to grab a large blue rubber band, gauze, anti-septic, a needle, and a bottle of some kind of medication. Even though he was lying on the table with a serious injury, he couldn't help but notice how attractive the nurse was. She was thick as hell and curvy, just how he preferred. It was also a plus that she was extremely pretty in the face. Her hair was straight and pulled into a low ponytail at the back of her head and she looked damn good in her powder blue scrubs. He couldn't help but notice that her ass was nice, round, and enticing to him.

Ramello forced himself to look away, his mind immediately going to the gutter. The nurse turned around as she put a pair of blue nitrile gloves on, and then grabbed the rubber band. "Alright, Dixon, this is going to be a bit uncomfortable, but I need to stop this bleeding so we can get this stitched up, okay? It's gonna be tight..." She said as she carefully lifted his thigh, slipped the band beneath it, and tied it above the area where the cut was.

Just as I'm sure that pussy is, Ramello thought. His face twisted at the pinch that came from the tightness of the band.

"Are you feeling light-headed at all?" Dominique looked at Sierra who was handing her a paper cup filled with cool water. "Grab me a straw, please."

Sierra grabbed a bendy straw from a cup near the water

jug, handed it to her, and watched Dominique carefully put the straw in the cup before putting it to Ramello's lips.

He shook his head in response and wrapped his big lips around the straw, quickly sucking down the cool water. The entire time he drank the water, the two locked eyes, unintentionally holding one another's gaze. Sierra watched them, a small smirk pulling at her lips. She knew her friend was a relatively shy woman, eye contact was something that wasn't big on her list, especially not with a stranger. Yet, there she was making googley eyes with an inmate. How she was seeing, it was only going to be a matter of time before she would change her tune. All it was going to take was the right one.

Ramello finished the water and Dominique put the cup down, grabbed pieces of gauze, pressed them to the open wound, and wiped down the areas around it.

"Ssss!" Ramello flinched at her touch.

"Sorry," she said. "Just bear with me a little longer and I will give you something to numb the pain while I stitch you up, okay?"

Staring up at the ceiling, Ramello nodded and took a deep breath to mask his pain. The longer he sat there, the more pain he felt. His mind was reeling as the nurse worked on his leg. Her touch was light, soft, and experienced, as she grabbed a small bucket with warm water, anti-septic soap, and a small wash cloth and cleaned the blood from his leg.

Unexpectedly he felt his dick begin to harden as she cleaned him. Her soft touch along with the warmth of the water and her kind demeanor had him rising, unable to hide the growing bulge in what was left of his pants. A part of him felt embarrassed that he was reacting that way in response to being cared for, but at the same time, how could he not? He was in a room with two good-looking women who were hovering over him, touching him, and essentially catering to his needs.

Looking away from the ceiling, he looked at the female officer who was still in the room with them and found her staring straight at the growing tent in his pants. She was biting her lip, staring unabashedly. He felt his skin grow hot and his dick only grew stiffer, throbbing with desire as images of both the good-looking women with their pretty, full lips wrapped around the shaft of his dick flooded his mind.

The nurse cleared her throat and her eyes flickered up to Sierra. "Thanks, Ms. Jones. That's all I needed." She dismissed the woman.

Sierra pursed her lips and narrowed her eyes at her but said nothing and moved toward the door. "Oh, okay. You want him for yourself, I get it. I'll get out of your hair."

Dominique looked up at her with a glare, annoyed that she was putting her friend out like that. She was pushing the whole fucking with an inmate thing like she hadn't already told her that she wasn't willing to risk her license. She just couldn't have her friend in there making the man uncomfortable by staring at his dick. It was unprofessional and quite frankly, awkward. She rolled her eyes when Sierra flipped her the bird before slipping out of the door.

"Sorry about that." She mumbled before resuming her cleanup of the man's leg.

"It's all good." Ramello's voice was deep and his eyes were low with desire. He was enjoying being handled with care by the attractive nurse and now that they were alone, he felt more comfortable getting in his mode. There was something about the way that she was looking into his eyes that let him know that if he was to shoot his shot, that she just might pick up what he was putting down. "Sorry about *that.*" He looked pointedly at the large tent in his pants.

The sweet giggle that left her pretty pink lips was everything he needed to hear and didn't even know it. "It's natural. Nothing I'm not used to." A small smile pulled at her lips as she picked up a needle and began loading it with medicine.

"Yeah... I'm sure you are used to makin' niggas hard and shit." Now more relaxed, he put his hands behind his head and watched her intently as she continued patching him up. The throbbing of his dick had him completely distracted from the pain in his leg. It had begun to go numb anyway from the rubber band slowing the circulation.

Dominique giggled again and positioned herself over his leg so that she could inject him with a numbing anesthesia so she could stitch his leg back up. "I think you're just saying that." She couldn't help but glance at the tent again, his length was straining against the fabric. It looked big and her mind immediately began to wonder what it *really* looked like. "That's just your adrenaline pumping." She tried to come up with an excuse to keep her from feeling flattered.

"Mmm, maybe..." Romello licked his lips and smirked as he watched her turn to grab more gauze and noticed the wave of her hand as she fanned herself. She was just as hot and bothered as he was. "I think it's cause how good you're taking care of me."

She laughed as she turned back to him. "You're funny. You have a habit of flirting with every nurse you come in contact with?" She looked over her shoulder at him.

"Only the pretty ones." He gave her a boyish grin, showing off a nice set of white teeth.

She waved him off, and turned back around, chuckling and reminding herself that he was an inmate. She was used to being flirted with when it came to patients, whether it was in the jail, or at her second job at the hospital. It came with the job, but it was rare that she entertained the flirting. For some reason, though, she found herself entertaining Ramello and his antics. It was so natural, she couldn't stop herself and that threw her for a loop a bit.

"Alright, let me numb you up a little bit so we can sew you up and get you outta here."

"Damn, you tryna get rid of me already?" Ramello teased.

"You want to bleed out?" She bent over his leg and injected him with the anesthetic.

"Aiight, I get your point." He chuckled then went quiet and allowed the nurse to do what she needed to do.

"Okay," she pulled the rubber band loose and then grabbed her needle and surgical thread. "Big pinch, take a deep breath... Good."

Ramello's face was stoic as Dominique gracefully and fairly quickly stitched him up. He didn't feel too much, only the slight tugging that came from the thread as she weaved it through his skin. The cut stretched across nearly the entire diameter of his thigh. He would be feeling that for a few weeks.

"And done." Dominique smiled down at her handiwork and gently rubbed Melly's lower thigh. "How are you feeling?"

"I've been worse." He shrugged and sat up on his elbows. "Thank you." He licked his lips, his eyes on her plump ass as she walked over to a cupboard and opened it where she grabbed an extra pair of pants and boxers. He wanted like hell to just be able to rub on the woman's phat booty, but he knew that was just the caged-up dog in him that was feeling the urge to mate.

"Of course," she smiled at him and met his eyes, approaching him with the clothing. She cleared her throat when she was back at his side. "You need help getting out the rest of those clothes and into these new ones?"

"If it's not too much to ask."

Dominique swallowed hard, her heart speeding up in her

chest. Of course, he was going to need her help after his injury, and he was also going to have to linger in the office for a bit until the numbing in his leg went away, even if it was in the infirmary part of Medical. She couldn't risk him walking around in the dorm and having him collapse because his thigh was numb. So, he would be spending a little bit of time with her that day. "No problem. Here, let me cut the other side off for you so we don't have to make you lift so much." She suggested and grabbed the scissors and cut the other side of his pants off of him from the pants leg up, and did the same with the boxers.

Her eyes nearly bulged out of her head when she removed the fabric from his nether regions. As soon as she exposed the bottom half of his body, Ramello's thick, hard dick went springing up landing against his bellybutton with an audible smack.

"Damn..."

A smug smirk was on Ramello's face as he watched the nurse eye his veiny dick with a look of awe on her face. His day had started rough. The last place he had expected himself to be was in the nurse's office because a fuck nigga had tried him. All the same, he liked the turn of events that his day had taken. He may have been injured, but he could tell the experience that came with the nurse who was caring for him was going to be worth it.

Nurse Dominique was looking and interested. He had a chance, and that's all he needed to know. If she was willing to go that far, he wanted to see just *how* far he could get her to go.

He watched her blink a few times before snatching her eyes away from his length. She turned to grab the bucket, a soiled washcloth that she used to clean blood from his thigh and dumped them in the sink. Ramello grabbed his dick in his hand and slowly began stroking it to her physique. The worst she could do was tell him to stop and put it away, or tell the officer to write him a Disciplinary Report for a B-11.

And Ms. Jones ain't gone be wit' that shit, anyways. His teeth were lodged into his bottom lip, the head of his dick leaking pre-cum in anticipation of her reaction to him stroking himself to her. It was a test to see how she would react.

Dominique turned around with fresh water and a clean washcloth and paused, heat lighting up her eyes when she saw him fisting his erection. She bit her lip, shook her head slightly, and chuckled before walking back to his side. "You're trouble, aren't you, Dixon?"

"I may be." His voice was low and thick with lust, thoroughly enjoying the direction that their interaction was going. He liked that she hadn't gotten offended and hadn't told him to stop. He continued pleasuring himself as she dunked the cloth into the soapy water and then rung it out over his thighs and pelvis. His eyes fluttered at the warmth of the water, and then the nurse's soft touch as she scrubbed the blood that remained on the rest of the skin that had trickled down his legs and over his pelvis.

"Hmmm..." she curiously met his eyes.

"Do you like trouble, Nurse Dominique?"

"I try to avoid trouble as much as possible." Her eyes drifted back down to Ramello's dick in his hand. "It usually has a way of finding me, though..."

Ramello grunted softly. "Trouble's good sometimes. It can be *fun*." He increased the speed of his strokes.

"That may be true, but it also comes with consequences." She met his eyes again to let him know that she was serious. Still, she continued washing his lower half, cleaning both of his legs and around his pelvis, avoiding his dick and the base of his shaft, the places she wanted to touch the most, but was fighting hard against the urge to do so.

"Only if you get caught." He was enticing her. Ramello stopped his stroking and held his dick by the base of his shaft and waved it at her.

Dominique found Ramello to be extremely attractive. He was tall, in shape by what she could tell from the two defined abs that peeked from underneath his shirt, and by how toned his legs were. His dick was the definition of edible, like her favorite Snicker's bar and she couldn't help the dirty way she was imagining slurping him up for her own pleasure. The fact that she wasn't supposed to even be watching him pleasure himself, and then asking her to participate had her clit thumping against the seat of her panties.

Wordlessly, Dominique dipped the cloth back into the soapy water, rug it out a bit, then with it still in hand she wrapped it around Ramello's dick and slowly cleaned it for him.

Ramello inhaled sharply, his excitement growing when she gave in and *touched* him. "Damn..." His eyes shut and he dropped his head back in pleasure. Again, the touch was soft as she massaged his length with the cloth barrier, but it still felt good because it was a touch other than *his*. It had been seven long years since he had an intimate touch from a woman, so the moment that he was having with the nurse was everything that he needed and more.

"You like that?" Her voice was low and seductive as she watched the pleasure play out on his face.

"Hell yeah," he groaned. His hips were thrusting against her hand.

Dominique removed the towel, gripped Ramello's dick in both her hands, and began jacking it with her soapy, gloved hands, twisting them in opposite directions. Her grip was firm, yet soft at the same time, her small hands expertly massaging his girth.

"Ugh!" He groaned again when she stilled one hand, gripping the base of his shaft, focusing her attention on the head with short, controlled strokes. Pressure was building in his core as he felt himself about to cum.

It had only been a few minutes that she was stroking his length for him, but he was so worked up with excitement that he was struggling to prolong the moment like he so desperately wanted to.

"Cum for me, Dixon." She cooed to him.

"Fuuuuck." His entire body shook as his dick erupted, sending spurt after spurt of cum shooting every which way. He had never cum so hard in his life. "Goddamn..." He was breathless when he spoke.

"Mhmm... let it allll out." A satisfied grin was on her face, and her pretty almond-shaped eyes almost looked closed as she looked down at him. Once she was sure that she had milked him of every drop he had, Dominique let go of his shaft, grabbed the bucket and washcloth again, and began cleaning up the mess that her patient had made.

"Shit, girl... I needed that." Ramello shook his head in disbelief and laughed. He almost felt like he was in a dream and was waiting for himself to wake up, but it was very much his reality.

"I'm sure you did." Dominique giggled as she bent over to clean up the drops of cum that had landed on the floor around the medical table.

Ramello lazily turned and looked at Dominique with hooded, lust-filled eyes. "You know you just fucked up, right?"

For a few moments she didn't reply, just continued cleaning. "Yeah, I knew you were trouble..." She shook her head at herself.

"As long as you know."

Chapter 2

"Tell me what happened! Was it big?!" Sierra's voice sounded loud in Dominique's ear as she switched on the lights. They had just walked into her town-home. She had completed her twenty-four-hour shift and would have the next day to relax before she got right back to it. Dominique was extremely tired but had decided to give her friend a call before she turned it in for the day. It was a bit past eight in the morning, so she was sure that her friend was getting ready to start her shift at the prison again.

Her last four hours at the hospital went by fairly quickly, she was only filling in for a few hours considering the hospital had been short-staffed. She was paid well, so she didn't mind doing the extra time, but she paid for it when it came to her sleep schedule. Exhaustion wasn't half of what she felt.

Now she was on the phone with her best friend who didn't want to do anything but gossip. "I don't know what you're talking about."

"Bullshit! That nigga was giddy as a muthafucka when he came out of that damn office. I know who Ramello is. He's no regular nigga. Ain't that friendly, either."

"Who?"

"Ramello. That's Dixon. It's what they call him 'round the compound." Sierra explained. "I've never seen that nigga crack so much as a *smile*. As hard as he tried not to let it show, I know when a nigga just got some pussy."

Dominique imagined her friend wagging her finger in the air and rolling her neck and busted out laughing at her friend's assumption. Though she wasn't too far off, she was still wrong. She stepped into the bathroom, put her phone on speaker, and sat it on the sink so she could continue talking while she stripped out of her clothes. "Just because you be handing out pussy to them inmates like its candy doesn't mean that I am, too."

"Then what *did* you give him, then, Mini, hmm?"

Dominique went quiet unable to help the smile that spread across her face as she replayed the memory of her stroking Ramello's dick until he came all over himself, her hands, the table, and the floor. "Okay, it was a hand job, but that was it."

"I fuckin' knew it! What did I tell you? What did I fuckin' tell you?" She could tell that her friend was just as ecstatic about the situation as she was.

"Yeah, yeah, yeah... I know... I didn't expect it to happen so soon, though." She shook her head and looked into the bathroom mirror and noticed that her normally dull eyes were bright with excitement.

"Tell me! Was it big? Did you wanna suck it? How did you end up with his dick in your hands? Give me all the details! I'm dying to know. Dixon's fine ass looks like he got the type of dick that just melts in your mouth–"

"Chillll, we are *not* about to talk about this man right now, but to answer your question, *yes,* it was big. Yes, I wanted to suck it. But that's probably as far as this shit is finna go. That's it, that's all. I don't need no more trouble and that man screams nothing but trouble." She shook her head already having made up her mind.

"Aw, you suck. If you were gonna go that far, you might as well had went all the way and fucked him to get the shit out of your system. You're real naivé if you think that he's not gonna want some more after all of that. Welcome to the dark side sister." The dark chuckle that met Dominique's ear made her shiver.

There was something about her friends' words that resonated with her spirit in a way that she didn't understand but her body reacted to it. It seemed significant.

HOURS LATER, Dominique rolled over onto her back in her bed and stretched. She had just woken up from a deep and much-needed rest and still, she felt a bit fatigued. With a yawn, she grabbed her cell phone to check her messages and social media pages. She was typically swamped with commitments, leaving little room for socializing, which meant that not many people stayed in regular contact with her. Nevertheless, she maintained a connection to her small circle of friends and the wider world through social media.

She opened the Facebook app to quite a few notifications so she clicked on the little bell icon, and her heart began thudding in her chest when at the very top sat a friend request from none other than, "Ramello Dixon." She said his name out loud and then clicked on his profile picture.

Dominique rolled her eyes and chuckled to herself as Sierra's words echoed in her head. *You're real naive if you think that he's not gonna want some more after all that. Welcome to the dark side sister.* For the next few minutes, she scrolled through the man's profile getting a feel for him. From motivational quotes to pictures of himself, and thoughtful think pieces, there wasn't anything that gave her any real red flags. Other than the fact that he was an inmate with access to social media, everything else about his page seemed to be relatively normal.

So, she accepted his request.

Almost moments later, she received a message from him on the Messenger app.

Ramello: Wassup, shawty...

Dominique: I can't believe you found me on here...

Ramello: I'm a man of many means. I know more about you than you know.

Dominique: Is that supposed to flatter me?

Ramello: Not, really. I'm just letting you know wassup.

Ramello: I don't like to do this texting thing, though. Video call?

Before she could reply with an answer, a video call was coming through her line. She thought about not answering because she was far from prepared. She wasn't dressed, her hair a mess, and the room was dark thanks to her drawing the blackout curtains she had installed to block out the sun to help her sleep during the day after working all night. She answered the call in the dark anyway.

"It's kinda rude to ask someone a question and not give them an opportunity to answer, don't you think? I could have been busy after all." She could see Ramello sitting in what was clear to be his cell.

"My bad. Are you busy? I can't see you." He sounded disappointed.

"Busy? Not quite. I just woke up from a nap after a twenty-four-hour shift. I'm still tired. I'm not presentable."

"Damn... my fault. Want me to call you back?" She watched as he uncomfortably scratched the back of his neck.

She could tell that he had just gotten a haircut thanks to the sharp lineup on his fade. A part of her felt like he had gotten the cut for her, but then she figured that maybe she was just being delusional and wanted him to have got a haircut for her. "Yeah, I'm going to rest up some more and I'll hit you when I'm awake and decent."

"Bet. Sweet dreams, Dominique."

"Goodnight, Dixon."

Dominique ended the call, dropped the phone onto the bed, and bit back a smile. She didn't know what it was about the man that made her feel so euphoric. Maybe it was the fact that she was finally getting some attention from a man, something she had convinced herself that she didn't want or need. Though she didn't walk around with the *fuck niggas* sign plastered to her forehead, she was still guarded, and it made her feel damn good that he was interested.

With a content sigh and a soft smile, she rolled over onto her stomach and drifted off to sleep.

"MMM. OOH. AHH. FUCK." Soft moans fell from Dominique's mouth as her delicate fingers stroked in and out of her wet pussy as thoughts of Ramello plagued her mind.

She couldn't help but long to feel his thickness stretching out all of her holes and filling her up with hot, sticky loads of cum. With a whimper, the nurse pulled her fingers out of her wet pussy and stuck her middle and ring fingers in her mouth, sucking the juices them. A knock at the metal door pulled her from her nasty pleasure break.

Standing to her feet, Dominique quickly pulled her scrubs up and straightened herself out before shouting, "It's open!" She moved to the sink and washed her hands. She heard whoever had come in shut the door behind her and then quiet footsteps.

She turned around and gasped as she was lifted onto the countertop and a pair of thick lips enveloped hers. "I can't stop thinking about how hard you made me cum," he whispered in between her passionate kisses.

She recognized the voice as Ramello's and melted into his touch, her arms and legs wrapping around his neck and waist. "I can't either," she said breathlessly when he began trailing his kisses down her neck.

"I need you."

Dominique's eyes rolled into the back of her head when he roughly bit her shoulder while one of his hands stuffed themselves into her bra, and the other into her scrubs and began playing in her wetness. "Then you can have me."

"You was playin' in this pussy in here, weren't you?" His voice nearly came out as a growl.

"Huh?" She was confused as to how he could have possibly known that, but she couldn't think straight thanks to his thick fingers massaging her clit.

"I can smell you. The smell of you drivin' a nigga crazy."

He removed his fingers from her pussy and put them to his nose and inhaled deeply. "Fuck, I need to taste you."

Frantically, they began pulling her scrubs and panties down her thighs. They weren't even all the way off her feet when Ramello's face was buried in her pussy, sucking attentively on her clit, and lapping up the juices that leaked from her middle.

"Oh, my G—" Dominique's mouth dropped, and formed an 'O.' "Sssss. W—wait! Ramel—Mmmm...the door. What about the door?"

"Ms. Jones got it." Ramello made loud kissing and sucking sounds on her clit, and licked her slit. "She's watching out for us. We good." He turned his head sideways and began wagging his tongue back and forth across her clit in rapid motions.

"Ooooh, just like that, don't stop." Both of Doninique's hands were on the back of his head. Her breath caught in her throat, and her brow creased. "Fuck!" He pulled her to the edge of the countertop and repeatedly fucked her bright pink hole with his tongue.

"Mmm..." Ramello was ravishing her, moaning as he thoroughly enjoyed feasting on her femininity. It had been far too long, and she tasted far too good.

Right before she was about to cum, Ramello stood to his feet and whipped his throbbing dick out of his pants, and held it by the base. "Suck it."

Wordlessly, Dominique slid off the counter and immedi-

ately dropped to her knees, and started circling the tip of her tongue around the head of his dick. She looked up at him from under her long, pretty eyelashes meeting his eyes and she slowly took his dick into her warm, wet mouth until it hit the back of her throat.

Ramello's head dropped back and a low groan escaped the back of his throat. He'd been waiting to feel his dick being massaged by the inside of her mouth from the moment he had laid eyes on her pretty lips. He couldn't help himself when he grabbed the back of her head and pushed it further down her throat until she gagged violently and then let up. After allowing her to catch her breath momentarily, he groaned and forced her head back down on his dick again, fucking her face forcefully until bubbles and spit dripped from her chin and onto the floor. Only the sounds of her slurping, gagging, and his grunts were heard.

"Yeah, play wit' that pussy," he said when he looked down and found the nurse playing with her pussy while he fucked her throat. He wanted her to be dripping wet when he finally got to slide his dick inside of her. "Get up and lay on the table. I need this pussy, right now." He pulled out of her mouth and gestured with his head towards the medical table.

Together, the two shuffled over to the medical table, Dominique removing her shoes so she could get her pants off. Once her feet were free, she laid on her back on the table and spread herself wide showing Ramello just how wet and ready she was for him to fuck her. Her bare lips were puffy and swollen with arousal, coated in her wetness, the pheromones coming from her only driving the sex-starved man wild with desire.

Ramello slapped his throbbing length against her swollen clit that peeked out from its hood, pretty and begging for attention. "Pretty ass pussy..." He rubbed his length against the entire outside of her pussy, teasing her, loving the torturous moans that came from her.

"Please..." She begged, locking eyes with the man she'd been fantasizing about since they had encountered one another.

Finally lining his dick up with the entrance of her pussy, he was about to push into her when a loud ringing sound caused Dominique to jump out of her sleep and wake from the best wet dream that she had ever had.

"Fuck!" She kicked her feet, upset when she realized that it was only a dream. She turned off her alarm, threw her arm over her face, and whimpered. She desperately wanted the dream to have been real. It had been far too long since she had been fucked, and a good fucking was exactly what she needed to relieve her of the stress that she experienced daily thanks to her career choice.

It was then that Dominique realized that her friend may have been right after all.

Chapter 3

$\mathcal{R}$omello opened his eyes, awakening from the most intense dream he'd had in years, and couldn't ignore the throbbing of his dick. He had been dreaming about a very fulfilling and pleasurable sexcapade that he was having with the nurse that had given him a hand job when he had gone to Medical to get patched up from the cut in his thigh. He looked down at the tent in his pants and saw pre-cum leaking through his shorts and shook his head. He couldn't remember ever wanting to fuck a bitch as bad as he wanted to fuck the nurse that had him shooting cum the way she did that day in her office.

Best believe that right after he was returned to his cell, he went straight to the net and started digging for what he could find out about the woman. He didn't want to put anyone in his business, but one thing he knew was that Ms. Jones, the C.O. who worked the booth most days, seemed to be a close friend of the nurse. He had picked up on their friendly connection while they were in the office, and he knew that the woman had fucked with some GD-affiliated guy in the dorm next to his that he shopped with on the cans of tobacco from time to time. Sierra was her real name.

It was nothing for him to go to the man's Facebook page, and scroll through his friend's list to find her, which then led him straight to his target. He was disappointed to find that everything on her page was private, but he had gathered enough information about her thanks to her friend's page.

Sierra was a social media ass bitch, so she posted everything and often tagged Dominique in her posts when they hung together or found memes that reminded her of the nurse. It wasn't much for him to go by, but it was enough for him to get a good feel for her. Once he was satisfied with the information that he had gathered about her, he sent her a friend request.

He was disappointed that she hadn't wanted to talk to him when he tried to get her on the phone with him and he was beginning to think that he had come on too strong.

Deciding that he was ready to get up for the day, he made a plan to get back to the nurse's office so that he could see her. If she was willing to stroke his dick, she was fasho going to be willing to give him some pussy. He could tell that he was just going to have to be a bit more persistent when it came down to it with her. That much he could tell. She was a reserved thing but underneath her professionalism, he knew that there was a slut in her. His dream confirmed that to him.

Ramello took care of his hygiene for the day then proceeded to make his way to the flap of the booth where he saw Sierra sitting on her phone. He knocked on the window, causing her to look up at him. She smirked when he waved her over and gestured for her to put her ear to the flap. "Aye, I gotta go to medical, shawty."

"Why? Whatchu need from there? You hurt again?" She asked humor in her tone.

"Yeah, I think I busted my stitches open again." He lied.

The woman laughed. "You sure you really gotta go to medical? Nurse Dominique ain't workin' today." She informed him.

Damn! He thought to himself. "Who down there, right now?"

"A man." She laughed again.

Ramello stood up and waved her off. "Shit, wassup wit' you, then?" He asked instead, his mind going back to the way that she was eyeing his dick back in the office.

She laughed even louder and was her turn to wave him off. "Boy, bye. You ain't ready for me, yet. You'll know when we are ready for you." Then she walked away, leaving him there pondering about what she could have possibly meant by that. His dick jumped at the image of both the women on their knees as he stood over them jacking his dick, ready to feed both the nurse and the C.O. his cum.

These hoes playin' wit' me, he thought as he walked away from the booth and went back to his cell. He walked in and Haniyf was kicked back on his bunk reading, *Despite The Odds: Let The Streets Choose by Juhnell Morgan.*

"As-salamu-alaikum," he greeted him.

Haniyf turned the page without looking up. "Wa-alaikum-salam."

Must be good. I'ma read it when he finish. Ramello pulled his phone from its hiding place and checked his messages for the first time that day.

His eyes widened as he saw that he had a video from Dominique and from what he could see in the thumbnail of the video, he saw nothing but ass and bare skin. He turned to his bunkmate who was lying on his cot scrolling on his phone. "Aye bruh, I need some privacy."

Haniyf nodded and got up off his cot and began heading for the door.

"Put some tissue in the do' for me. 'Preciate it."

Once the door was closed, Ramello got comfortable on his cot, whipped his dick out, and played the video the sexy nurse had sent to him. "Goddamn." He bit his bottom lip when he saw the woman laying in her bed with a clear dildo fucking her pussy.

"Oh, Melly, I wish it was you and not this fucking dildo stroking the insides of my tight wet walls right now. I want that big chocolate dick pounding my pussy. Are you gonna fuck this needy pussy for me, baby? It's been so long since I had some dick. You see how fuckin' horny you got me, right now? You see how creamy this pussy is for you?"

"I knew yo fine ass was fuckin' nasty," he mumbled to himself out loud, he dipped his hand in a jar of Vaseline and scooped some out before wrapping his hand around his length and fisting his throbbing erection in pace with the way Nurse Dominique was fucking herself with the dildo. The last thing he had expected to wake up to was a video of her fucking herself and telling him how much she wanted him.

The video cut to a new scene of the nurse sitting in a chair, the angle was low probably from her phone sitting on the floor as she rode the dildo reverse cowgirl style, her phat ass bouncing uncontrollably in pace with the R&B love song that she had playing in the background. It made him only that much harder for her.

Her pretty Mahogany skin was shone and dripped with sweat as she put in the work to fuck herself and all he could imagine was that it was him that she was riding. She was showing off her skillset to him and everything that she was doing in the video was exactly what he wanted and needed in that moment.

Now that he knew what she was capable of and exactly what it was that she had to offer, he *needed* it. All of her.

Moments later she was showing him a new angle and she had one foot up on a chair while she rode the dildo. *"Bring that dick back."* She said when the dildo came loose from the chair and moaned loudly. When she caught her rhythm again, the sight of her titties, belly, and all of her rolls jiggling turned him on immensely and had him cumming before the video had even ended. "Uggggh." He squeezed his eyes shut tightly, riding out yet another orgasm that had him erupting wild. "Whew." He had broken out into a sweat.

Closing out of the video, he took a picture of the cum all over his arm and stomach then cleaned up his mess. Finished, he called Dominique on Messenger.

"Hello," a sweet voice answered followed by a giggle.

"Goddamn, mama, you got a nigga worked up like a mufucka. Why you such a fuckin' tease, huh? Check your messages. Look what you made me do." His tone was smug yet satisfied.

"Oh, look at that mess... I wish I was there to lick it up." He could hear the desire in her voice.

"I wish you was, too. I wanna know when you gonna let me feed it to you."

"Mmm, I haven't quite figured that part out just yet. I want you... but like I said I know you're trouble. We can have fun like this, though, right? I like the attention and I make you cum. That's fair isn't it?"

"Fair? Nah, that's teasing. I want *you.* All of you. I wanna put this dick in yo stomach. What we've done so far is cool, but I want more. I want the real thing. Them holes is what I'm after."

She moaned on the other end of the phone. "I hear you, but I ain't tryna get caught up. I worked too hard for my license..." He could tell that she was still guarded even though they had already crossed lines.

"I mean, shit, we already crossed lines. What's a few more? I ain't no hoe ass nigga. What happens between us, stays between us." He attempted to reassure her.

"That all sounds good, but that's a little difficult to do in a prison. We may get away with it a time or two, but I couldn't see us getting away with it very long."

"How about we just worry about that when that time gets here? Like you said in that video, you want me pounding that pussy. Let me scratch that itch for you, baby. Fuckin' wit' a nigga like me... I can make your wildest fantasies a reality." He felt his dick growing hard all over again at the thought. He meant every word of what he was saying.

"I'll think about it..." He could still hear the hesitance in her voice but he would take it. It was better than a no, that was for sure.

"When you come back to work?" He asked.

"Tomorrow."

"What time you usually start working?" He pried.

"When I get there." She giggled again.

"Aiight, shawty..." He smirked. While he felt that she was easy, he knew that there was a lot more to her than she was letting on. Access to her body was one thing, but access to the *real* her was going to be harder than he thought.

Not only did he want inside of her pussy, but he wanted inside of her head, too. The more he saw from her, the more he found himself attracted to her in more than one way. There was just something about her.

Chapter 4

"You know Ramello was looking for you today, right?" Sierra asked as she took the wine glass that Dominique held out for her. She had stopped by her best friend's house after work so that they could catch up in person.

Dominique laughed, her mind immediately flashing back to the conversation that she had with him earlier that day. "I'm sure he was."

Sierra tossed her braids over her shoulder and pointed a finger at her friend. "Mmm, what does that mean? Talk!" She demanded.

"Why it gotta mean something? Damn! I made the man nut. Of course, his ass gonna be lookin' for me." She said as if she was stating the obvious and took a sip of the sweet red wine that she and her friend were sipping on.

"Bull. Shit. You not telling me something." She hit her friend on her thick thigh. She was nosey as fuck.

Dominique sighed, placed her wine glass on the table, tucked her leg underneath her, and angled her body toward her friend. Her feet were bare and she was in a pair of boy shorts, and a white tank top, and her hair was in a messy bun on the top of her head. They were in the living room of her nicely decorated townhome. There was an earthy feel to the decor. Plants and pictures of plants were all over, strategically placed, and each of them bright green and comforting to the woman. Green, cream, and grey were the color scheme of the furniture in the room.

Sierra loved being there because it was always comforting to her, and she often would come over just to crash on her couch because it was so peaceful in her environment. It was one thing that she loved about Dominique; she was often a beacon of peace for her and her home embodied that for her.

"Actually, there is something that I need to tell you." She looked at her friend with what she thought was an intimidating look. "He found me on Facebook because of you, you know?"

Sierra burst out laughing. "That man wasted no time! Good for him." She giggled deviously. "I *told* you all it was gonna take was one and now that nigga on yo ass! You wanna fuck him don't you, Mini? It's okay, go ahead and admit it."

Dominique said nothing, instead opting to grab her wine

glass and take a sip of her drink. "Of course, I do." She rolled her eyes and poked her bottom lip out in a pout. "I'm scared I'ma get in trouble, though."

"The possibility of getting caught is what makes it *exciting.* You should just be bad for once! Let go and let God! Ain't no tellin' what will come from this shit!" Sierra was giddy to be having such a conversation with her boring best friend. She had been waiting for the day that Dominique let loose. The woman was all work, no play, and Sierra l hated that for her. She wanted her friend to be happy and knew that the touch and attention of a man was exactly what she needed to let her hair down.

Dominique shrugged, contemplating what she would say next. "Let's say I do fuck this guy... how would that even work?"

"That's easy! The nigga just got his leg cut open. It won't look suspicious if I just bring his ass back there to you. Y'all do what y'all do, then I'll just bring his ass back." Sierra suggested as if it was that simple and took a large gulp of her wine. She would be needing another cup soon.

"What about Daniel, though?" He was the guard that normally stood outside of the door when she was inside with the inmates.

"He ain't gonna say shit. I'm fuckin' to keep him quiet about some other shit I got going on. You straight."

Dominique shook her head at her friend. "Who *aren't* you fuckin'?"

"Ramello." She chuckled darkly and brought her glass to her lips again.

"You ain't shit." Dominique laughed and held her cup out for her friend to clink against hers.

"So... tell me now... is tomorrow the day?" Sierra wiggled her eyebrows with a grin.

Dominique locked eyes with her friend and almost couldn't take her seriously with the mischievous glint in her eyes and she gave in. "Fuck it. Yeah... tomorrow is the day."

Sierra jumped up, squealed, and did a dance. One would have thought *she* was the one planning to fuck the inmate the next day. "Okay! Okay! Okay! You just have him come to Medical like he did today and then I'll bring him back. You ain't gotta worry about Daniel. I'll keep him busy while you do what you gotta do." She explained as she sat back down. "I'm so proud of you for putting on your big girl panties and having some fun for once. You're gonna love that prison dick." She said dreamily.

"You are something else, man." Dominique chuckled. "I can't believe I'm really sitting her talking to you about this..."

"Get used to it sister. You'll be hooked! My only piece of advice... *Do not catch feelings for that nigga.*" She emphasized.

NERVOUSLY, Dominique sat in her car in the prison parking lot as she looked down at the message she had typed up on her phone. She'd been anxious all night, up thinking about the plan she and Sierra had to bring Ramello down to her office so she could finally act on the nasty thoughts she'd been having about him.

That shit sounds crazy when I even think about it, she thought to herself.

Had she really made plans to have sex with an inmate, something she knew that if any of her higher-ups found out about, she was surely to be fired and would lose her nursing license? Was some prison dick really worth it? She didn't know, but what she *did* know was that she wanted to cum all over it.

Even if it was just once...

One time won't hurt... Yeah, I can do that. She had to give herself a pep talk, then hit send on the message.

Dominique: Let Sierra know you need to come to medical.

She twiddled her fingers nervously, stopping only to pat her back packet to make sure the three condoms she had stashed there hadn't fallen out. Her phone vibrated and she looked at the screen.

Ramello: Bet!

Dominique got out of her car, closed the door behind her, and headed in. Ten minutes later, she was pacing in her office when Sierra's familiar rhythmic knock signaled that she was outside, and with her, Ramello. Dominique walked over to the door and opened it for him to step inside.

"Y'all have fun, ya hear?" All Ramello and Dominique could see was Sierra's red-painted lips poking through a small gap in the door before she closed it.

Ramello looked down at Dominique with humor in his eyes. "What's up wit' yo homegirl."

She giggled and rolled her eyes playfully. "She's a nut job, that's what."

"Seems like it..." Ramello walked closer to her until he had her backed against a filing cabinet. "So wassup? You summonin' a nigga and shit. You been thinkin' bout what we talked about?"

"I have actually... That's why you're here, obviously..." She was getting nervous again as he towered over her and her nipples began turning into hard peaks.

He grabbed one of her hands that was dangling at her side and placed it on the bulge against his thigh. "I'm tryna put this dick in your stomach for real."

Then he took her lips, kissing her deeply.

A whimper left her as he reduced her to nothing but a pool of need. His lips felt soft against hers, causing her to fall further under the spell he was putting her under. She mewled softly when he gently slipped his tongue between her lips and explored every inch of her mouth.

Her head spun, making her feel as if she was being thrown into a different dimension. *What in the actual fuck?*

No man had ever made her feel that way.

She gasped, trying to catch her breath when he pulled his mouth from hers.

"You gonna let me do that?" He asked in between kisses that he trailed down her neck.

"Let you do what?" Suddenly, she couldn't remember what they had talked about.

He chuckled against her skin and pulled her harder against his bulge as he ground against her, needing friction. "Put this dick in your stomach."

She bit her lip and nodded. "Yes."

As soon as she said it, he kissed her and wrapped his arms around her. His hands reached around to cup her round cheeks. One of them moved down further, sliding down into her scrubs and underneath her panties, then down the crack of her ass. His fingertips came to a rest at the entrance of her pussy from behind and he groaned into her mouth.

She's so fucking wet.

He walked them over to the medical table, placed her on it, wheeled the nurse's stool over in front of her, and sat in it. She watched his every move, breathing heavily in anticipation of what he was about to do next. He gingerly removed her scrub bottoms and panties. She didn't miss it when he slipped her black lace panties into his pocket. Her stomach lurched with need when he grabbed her by her thick thighs and spread her wide. The hunger in his face had her eyes fluttering, trying to blink away her desire that was clouding her vision.

Eyeing her sex, he licked his lips and hummed. "Mmm. Mmm. Mmm. Look at that lil pussy drippin' for me."

She was so pretty down below. The brown folds of her labia looked inviting as they glistened with her excitement. Her entrance was a bright pink, and he damn near started salivating.

Pushing her thighs up, he locked eyes with her again.

"Hold 'em back."

Dominique did as she was told, and he wasted no time pulling her to the edge of the table and using his tongue to lick up her drippage.

"Ahhh…" Her mouth dropped open upon his mouth making contact with her pussy.

Ramello slurped up her juices and groaned into her center in appreciation. He couldn't tell anyone how many times he had fantasized about the exact moment they were sharing. She tasted far better than he had ever imagined.

He kissed her clit, making her thighs jump, then sucked it lightly, and turned his head to plant a kiss on her lower lips causing her to moan softly.

He watched her face as he started flicking his tongue quickly and gently back and forth across her clit. With another hum against her flesh, he was pleased when she pushed her scrub top and bra up to free her voluptuous assets.

He moaned in pleasure again, watching her tweak her nipples. She had small dark brown areoles, and her nipples were thick and hard. He couldn't wait to have them in his mouth. He hadn't even been inside of her yet and she already had him ready to bust in his pants.

He had never been so horny in his life.

So fuckin' pretty. He couldn't get over her beauty…the way her face contorted, her stomach heaved, and how she moaned his name...

He was positive that he would never be able to get over that fact *and* the fact that he was finally able to have a piece of her.

"Shit, baby. You're gonna make me cum." Her hands were still gripping her thighs, holding them back as he licked her to oblivion.

His lips were wrapped around her clit, sucking on it. He looked up, met her eyes again, and sucked harder.

He liked that she was watching him just as much as he was watching her. Something about it let him know she wasn't shy about the illicit nastiness that they were doing and were about to do. It was a completely different demeanor than she had a few minutes prior.

With a wink, he sent her plummeting off the face of the Earth, exploding in his mouth. Her body shook so hard it shook his big frame, too.

He caressed the underside of one of her ass cheeks that hung off the edge of the table. "Mmhm, that's it. Cum in my fuckin' mouth."

She let go of her thighs and pushed his head away because

it felt like he had no intentions of letting up on her clit anytime soon.

"Shiiit, okay. Ah, too sensitive." She let out a shaky laugh.

He sat back with a smirk and licked his lips. "Damn, that pussy is too good."

Dominique leaned forward and sensually swiped her tongue across his lips, tasting herself on him.

He groaned, his dick throbbing painfully in his boxers, longing to be inside her. He found the fact that she tasted herself on his lips to be extremely sexy.

Her hands went to his waistband, working to free him from his prison-ordered shorts. "I can't wait to taste your cum."

He bit his lip, watching her slide off the table and drop to her knees. He reached out to cup both of her little, pretty titties in his hands while she pulled his hard dick from his pants.

Ramello grinned and cupped his hand around the back of her neck, pulling her face toward his dick. "Get to it, then."

She said nothing else and took the thick head of his dick into her mouth, looking deep in his eyes. His mouth parted slightly as she slowly twirled her tongue around the mushroom-shaped tip. She had to open her mouth wide to even take another inch, but it wasn't anything she couldn't handle.

"Damn, you look so pretty with my dick in your mouth." He sounded as though he was in awe.

Dominique moaned in response, using both her hands to fist the rest of his length. Bending over her while she sucked him, he trailed one of his hands down behind her, sliding to the crack of her ass again until his middle finger came to a rest at her asshole, rubbing it gently in slow circles.

"Thank you," she said through a moan.

For a few minutes, Dominique sucked the prison inmate sloppily, losing herself in the feeling of his thickness massaging the inside of her throat.

"Get up and back on the table. I can't wait any longer. Hold them thighs back." he ordered her again, closing the space between them.

His eyes were on her wetness. Watching her open for him was like watching a lover peel away layers of restraint, each garment dropping to the floor in a tantalizing confession of readiness. He was dripping from the head of his dick in anticipation and licked his lips when he met her eyes, and she gave him a sexy smile. He loved the sight of her exposed stomach and was beyond grateful that she had confidently taken the initiative to raise her shirt and bra. Nothing turned him off quicker than Ebony BBW porn with a woman taking dick with her shirt on, and he didn't like it anymore in person. She had no way of knowing, but he had a thing for plus-size women.

He dipped his tongue in her navel, licked around, and traced a slow trail up between her titties, over her throat to her chin. Kissing her lightly on the lips, he pressed himself to her entrance. "If it's too much, let me know. Okay?"

Dominique's heart pounded in her chest, leaving her speechless but she nodded in agreement. Her breath was hitched in anticipation, each exhale a whisper of the pleasure to come.

Leaning forward, Ramello spit on her pussy, making her moan in response. She was already wet as hell on her own, but he was sure that he would need the extra lubrication. He was going to stretch her out and pound her pussy like she had asked him to in her video, and the last thing he wanted was for her to dry up on him.

Her mouth fell open as she gasped when he began entering her. She fisted her hands in his shirt, moaning when she felt him inside of her. The fact that she had brought condoms completely went out the window as she found herself caught up in *him*. He was filling her up and all she wanted was more.

"Fuck, I miss being in pussy." He groaned and leaned down and wrapped his lips around one of her nipples.

"Mmmm." She closed her eyes, as her defenses melted away, leaving her vulnerable and aching in the most exquisite way.

Buried completely within her, he stilled and looked into her eyes. "Good?"

She nodded. "Fuck me, Melly."

He groaned at her words. She had such a dirty mouth, and he loved that shit. He pulled out halfway, before slowly sliding back in. His face collapsed in pure pleasure. She was so warm wrapped around his length. She felt like a warm ass hug after being out in the cold all night. Warmth spread throughout his entire body as he found his rhythm stroking in and out of the woman that he had been having wet dreams about.

She yelped suddenly and her hand went flying to his stomach making him stop his motions.

"You okay?" His shirt was folded up against his stomach so that it wouldn't get wet, and his pants hung loosely around his knees.

She nodded. "Yeah, you're just…" she sucked in a breath and blew it out, "deep. That's all."

He smirked and resumed stroking.

"Oh, shit." It didn't take long for her to start feeling pleasure again.

She met his brown eyes. He winked at her again, and just like the last time, she lost it.

Her pussy convulsed and clenched tightly around his big dick, sucking him even deeper into her honey pot.

"Mmm, there you go. Look at you. Pretty as fuck, takin' all this dick like a good girl." He pressed a hand to her stomach, driving deeper into her.

"Oh, shit! It's so biiig." She whimpered in ecstasy. "I wanna feel it from the back," She said breathlessly, reaching a hand between them to rub her clit.

He pulled out of her and slapped his soaked dick against her clit before taking a step back. Biting his lip, he suppressed a laugh when she stood on shaky legs. "You aight?"

Dominique hopped down from the table and bent over it before she looked over her shoulder at him, arched her back, and gave him a sly smile. "I'm straight. Now, put that dick back in this pussy. Don't hold back."

Melly didn't hesitate to step forward and grab her by the hips, his touch igniting her skin, setting every nerve alight. "You sure about that?" He pushed his way back inside of her.

"Yesssss. Give it to me. Please!" She begged, her body trembling with lust.

Hearing her begging for more, brought out something in him that he hadn't ever experienced before. The fact that she was asking for more when he usually got the complete opposite, had excitement building deep inside of him. Most of the women that he had been with could never take his entire length. He was just going to add it to the list of shit that piqued his interest in her.

"Ahhhhh!" She screamed when he began pounding roughly in and out of her pussy.

"This what you wanted right?" He asked between strokes.

"Fuck, yes! Soooo, good."

He slapped her ass then spread her cheeks apart. Watching his dick disappear in and out of her wetness.

She hissed at the sting. taking the pussy beating that he was giving her. "Oh my—ah! That dick's in my stomach, baby!"

"Mmmmm. I'm bout to cum. Where you want it?" He popped his neck, bracing himself for what he knew was about to be the best orgasm of his life. His breaths were shallow as he held her by the waist pulling her back into him each time he plunged into her.

"Right there. I wanna feel you buss all in this pussy, baby."

"Ugh!" Releasing inside her without a second thought, he fell into her, unable to control his body as load after load came out in spurts. He thought he had died and re-visited Heaven.

"Mmmmmm." She moaned, a smile lighting up her face as she worked to catch her breath. She could feel his heart hammering in his chest as he leaned into her, trying to catch his own.

"Goddamn, girl," he groaned, pulling out of her.

Dominique giggled and looked at him over her shoulder. "Wow."

"Right." He grinned, taking a seat on the chair behind him.

A knock at the door caught his attention. It was Sierra. "Oooowwwee! That shit sounded like it was good!"

Dominique covered her face and shook her head as Ramello laughed. He found Sierra to be a funny ass woman. He could tell that she was having a good time. Her pussy was also something that he was curious about.

Moments later, the two then cleaned themselves up and made sure that they were presentable.

"We gotta do this again..." Ramello said looking down at Dominique with soft eyes. Her pussy had been amazing, and he needed some more. There was no way that they would be able to keep it to a one-time thing.

"I'll let you know when I'm ready..." Dominique replied in a soft and flirty voice.

Then she opened the door and Ramello left the room.

After he left, Dominique put her back to the door and slid down it with a grin on her face. The sex was great. Just like Sierra had promised, she was hooked.

Chapter 5

"The fuck you got goin' on with the nurse, man?" Haniyf asked early one morning after Ramello came strolling back into the room. He had watched intently as Ramello went to the door of the dorm and spoke with the C.O. briefly before returning to his cell.

"Fuck you mean? I'm injured. I gotta follow up with this cut." He replied nonchalantly.

"You were gone thirty minutes a couple of days ago. Ain't no way! You came back happy as a mufucka, too. You injured but ain't been actin' like it. Plus, everybody knows how that hoe Ms. Jones get down. She gotta be in on it." Haniyf was a smart nigga, very attentive, but it didn't matter. Ramello wasn't puttin' nobody in his business.

There was no way he was letting anybody in on what he

had going on with Nurse Dominique. The last thing he wanted anyone to think was that they could try his hoe. He wasn't sharing his pussy with another nigga in prison. He'd be damned!

"That shit all in yo head, bruh. I ain't got shit goin' on." He said dismissively and pulled his phone from his pocket.

"Yeah, aight, nigga..."

He was supposed to be meeting with Dominique that day, but she hadn't hit him up and let him know when he was supposed to be going down to the office. In fact he hadn't heard anything from her in over twenty-four hours and that was unlike her. It had him feeling some kind of way.

How the fuck she makin' plans and ain't een hit a nigga back? He decided to shoot her a text.

Ramello: You runnin' late today?

Dominique: Yeah. I just got here. Give me ten minutes then come on.

He felt better once she replied to his message. *She probably just had to handle some* shit, he figured.

Ten minutes later, as planned, Sierra popped the front door and stuck her head in the dorm.

"Dixon! Sick call!"

Inmates that had just seconds ago been playing spades, watching TV, and working out pushed up on her immediately.

"What's up, Ms. Jones?"

"Goddamn, Ms. Jones, wazzam?"

"That ass gettin' phat, girl," they said, vying for her attention. It was obvious to anyone with a pair of eyes that she loved every second of it…at least to Ramello, it was.

He did his best to play it cool and not seem too eager as he made his way to the front door where Sierra was posted surrounded by inmates.

Ramello shook his head as he approached. *These broke ass niggas be doin' the most. And this bitch…"*

Sierra was soaking up all the attention, laughing, and just as happy as ever. She saw him approaching, slapped the booth window twice, and signaled for the officer to pop the door.

"Alright y'all, I gotta go." The door popped, as she exerted pressure on it, swinging it open. Phat Wanny, a younger inmate, made a sudden dash for the door but she was quick to counter, firmly pushing him back into the dorm. Glancing over her shoulder to the door of the adjacent dorm, she saw a slim, dark-skinned inmate observing from the window. She was a vet and knew when someone was trying to grab a pack. She turned back to Phat Wanny "Gon' head on Jenkins. Ain't nobody got time for that, right now. I'll let you grab it when I come back."

Ramello stepped past Phat Wanny, into the sallyport.

Phat Wanny smiled. "Aight, I'll grab it when you come back. Soon as you open the door. Can't *wait* to grab it!"

"Boy, what the—" she slapped his arm, playfully. "You know what I'm talkin' bout!"

Everybody laughed.

"Now, move!" Sierra pushed him and slammed the door.

The booth officer popped the sallyport gate, and she headed out. "Always thinkin' nasty. Come on, Dixon."

Ramello walked out the sallyport, crossed the yard, and together they made their way up the walk, headed to Medical.

"Dixon, what be wrong wit' em?"

Ramello shrugged. "I don't know. Shiiid, them yo homeboys."

"Shiiiid!"

They both laughed.

At Medical, they made their way to Dominique's office, but she wasn't there. Ramello looked back at Sierra, and she waved him in.

"You good. Give her a minute. I'm finna go talk to Daniel."

"Who?"

Sierra tapped her head. "Thomas. I'm trippin'. You don't know that boy. Gon' head in, though. She comin'. And I'ma be right back. I got y'all."

Ramello stepped into the room and perched himself on the edge of the medical bed. Shortly after, Sierra entered, making her way to the sink where she scrubbed her hands meticulously. The door swung open again, allowing Dominique to slip through before she shut it with a soft click. As Sierra turned off the water, she pivoted to face the room, locking eyes with Ramello, who shifted his gaze between her and Dominique. A faint click announced the door was now locked.

Dominique spun around with a grin, meeting Ramello's puzzled stare, his forehead furrowed with a trace of suspicion.

"Someone was excited this morning," Dominique said with a giggle. "Come here," she beckoned him to her with the curl of her index finger.

He briefly looked over at Sierra.

"What? You don't want her to join in on the fun?" Her voice was low and seductive as she lowered herself to her knees. "I thought you wanted us both?" She questioned, pulling on his pants and freeing his already stiff dick.

It throbbed at the thought of having them both.

"I do... I just didn't expect y'all to be down with that." He licked his lips when Sierra came up behind him and trailed her tongue up the back of his neck.

"That's my best friend. I'm down for whatever when it comes to her," Sierra whispered seductively in his ear as a soft hand gripped the base of his dick and stroked it while Dominique sucked on the head of it. "You ain't the only one that can make fantasies come true."

It was then that it registered to him that he had been a topic of conversation when it came to the women.

Speechless and focused on the soft, wet tongue massaging the underside of his dick as Dominique sucked him. "Mmmm," Ramello moaned in response as his eyes fluttered closed in pleasure. He opened them again, and both women were on their knees before him. He bit his lip in anticipation as he watched Sierra take his dick from her friend's hand and immediately stuck his pulsating member in her mouth.

"Fuck." He groaned and put his arms behind his back as he allowed himself to indulge in the feeling of the two prison staff members pleasing him with their mouths. While they were normally in charge, here in this moment, he was the HNIC.

"Both of y'all, stick y'all tongues out." He instructed them and put his hands on the back of their heads and guided them to lick and suck along the sides of his dick in sync. "Goddamn, I love this shit," he said smugly. Taking his dick in hand, he began slapping them both in the face with his wet shaft, alternating between the two of them.

"Mmmmm," both Dominique and Sierra moaned and leaned into each other and kissed. Ramello's dick was hard as steel as he watched the nurse slip her long tongue into her best friend's mouth and began making out with her. He felt like a king watching Sierra rub on Dominique's phat ass, squeezing and kneading on it as they made out with one another. Words couldn't explain how turned on he was that he was actually living out one of his biggest fantasies in prison. He was in heaven.

He loved the way that Dominique's moans turned needy and grew louder as her friend began removing her clothing. They took their time, undressing and exploring one another until they were both naked. Ramello moved to the side and watched the two women stand from the floor and get on the medical table.

Dominique moaned and arched her back when Sierra dipped her head down and gently bit into her thick nipple, sending a jolt of both pleasure and pain throughout her body, then soothed it by swirling her soft, wet tongue around it repeatedly. While she did that, Sierra grabbed her friend by one of her thighs and lifted it, spreading the woman wide so that she could slip her thigh between hers and moved in close until both their bare pussies were kissing.

Slowly, Sierra began humping her, rubbing her shaved pussy all over her friend's waxed one. "Mmmm. Mmm. Mmm," Dominique moaned uncontrollably, her pretty face screwed up in pleasure. "I love rubbing pussies with you." She whimpered, moving her hips in sync with her friend's. They were both so wet that a thick gel had gathered between the two and only lubricated their pussies even more.

"Mmmm. I love it, too, baby. This pussy is so good! Come put it in my mouth while you suck on Ramello's dick." Sierra rolled off of her and switched places so she was lying on her back while Dominique hovered over her face. Once mounted, she slapped Dominique's pretty, Mahogany ass. Sierra's pussy dripped with need and lust as she took in the sight of Dominique's pretty pussy as she lowered it to her lips. Immediately, she began licking her pussy as if her life depended on it. Sierra's tongue touched and explored every single nook and cranny of her best friend's pussy.

While Dominique sat comfortably on Sierra's face, getting her pussy ate, she turned her attention to Ramello and put her face in his lap, spit dripping from her lips, onto his hard dick

"Ooow, y'all nasty." Ramello groaned loudly as his sexy nurse took his dick deep down her throat, swallowing him. "Yea, eat that dick up."

"Mhmm."

"You my nasty lil slut, Dominique?" Ramello took his dick from between her pretty lips, making her pout and whimper in disapproval. She wasn't done tasting him yet. He broke her from her thoughts when he slapped the length of his dick across her face to bring her attention back to him and not to her thoughts. He didn't want her to do any thinking, just what he said. He would do the thinking for her and all she had to do was agree.

"Yes." She replied simply, nodding her head as she eyed Ramello's dick in his hand, stroking it from base to tip, leaking his delicious pre-cum. She tried to lean and take it back into her mouth, but he slapped her, making her whimper and become wide-eyed and alert.

"Yes, what?" He questioned, teasingly rubbing the head of his dick against her bottom lip, leaving a small bit of his pre-cum on it as he did so. He smirked when she quickly darted her little pink tongue out and hurriedly licked up the tease of a drop.

"Yes, Daddy, I'm your nasty lil slut." The words were like music to his ears. He permitted her to take him back into her mouth, and groaned loudly when she sucked his dick to the back of her throat once more. "You like suckin' this chocolate dick while yo friend eats that pretty, tasty ass pussy, don't you, slut?"

With her head still bobbing on his dick and bouncing her pussy on Sierra's tongue, she moaned in agreement with his dick still in her mouth.

Beneath her, Sierra was in complete bliss as she gripped and caressed her friend's smooth ass and titties as she lapped at her pussy like a kitten drinking milk. She enjoyed the sweetness of both their pussy juices mixed from them rubbing pussies. Reaching a hand up, she spread her smooth pussy lips and began sucking on her clit intensely.

Ramello loved the way Sierra was making Dominique's whole-body tremble from pleasure as she brought her closer and closer to an amazing orgasm. She wanted it badly, too. The vibrations from Dominique's moans around his dick were driving him wild with lust. He needed his dick buried inside of her ASAP!

"Aight, come sit on this dick," Ramello demanded. "And turn around so that Sierra can lick and suck on yo clit and my balls." He said, his dick continuing to leak in anticipation.

He watched both women spring into action and get into position. Ramello traded spots with both of them and sat on the table while he supported Dominique by the waist. Sierra held his dick up and in place, as Dominique straddled him reverse cowgirl and lowered her tight pussy onto his length, making them all moan in blissful satisfaction.

Sierra's eyes were low and hooded as she watched Dominique stand on her feet and begin bouncing her tight snatch up and down on Ramello's dick. Dying to be filled by him next, her pussy leaked with longing, but that wasn't what she was there for. She was there as an extra mouth. In the meantime, she busied herself with licking and sucking on her friend's clit and Ramello's balls as Dominique rode him reverse cowgirl.

Dominique's pussy was leaving a thick layer of cream all over him with each drop of her pussy down on his dick. Her titties and stomach bounced as she did. It drove her wild when her friend licked her cream from Ramello's hard shaft as she fucked him.

From behind her, Ramello gripped Dominique's perky titties, pinching her nipples as she rode him. He was in pure ecstasy as they both sucked and fucked him so good that his toes curled. "Fuuck, this pussy got me 'bout to buss." He groaned, throwing his head back. "I'ma fill this pussy up."

Sierra couldn't help the pang of jealousy that flashed through her at the mention of him about to load her friend up with cum. Heat filled her eyes as she looked up from her position sucking on her clit and saw the pure pleasure that filled her eyes, and the sound of her moans as Romello dick stroked her to the finish line.

"Fuck! Daddy! I'm cumming all over your dick, Daddy!

Oh, my fuckinn' God!" Dominique did her best to keep her cries of pleasure down, her creamy pussy wetting his dick up.

"Yeah, baby! Cum with me. I'm 'bout to nut all up in this pussy!" Ramello groaned, holding the thick, sexy nurse by the waist and supporting her while she bounced on his big, black, dick.

"Yes! Yes! Yes! Cum—" She begged.

At her words, he grabbed her by the hips, holding her still, and began thrusting up into her pussy hard and fast until he exploded deep inside of her, his hot cum splashing hard against the walls of her tight pussy, filling her up to the hilt. "Auuuuggghhhhh." Ramelllo groaned as he emptied his balls into his favorite nurse.

Ramello was exhausted as the woman got off of him and he laid down on the table completely spent.

That was something that he could get used to.

Chapter 6

"**Y**ou still stickin' to that story that you not fuckin' with the nurse, huh?" Haniyf asked when Ramello came back from medical looking completely spent.

"Not right now, nigga." Ramello waved him off as he laid back down on his cot ready to take a nap. The last thing he had expected when got down to that office was for him to be pleased by *both* Dominique and Sierra, but he wasn't complaining about it at all. He had had a good time. A great time, actually. So much so that he was beginning to feel the ache in his thigh from having Dominique bouncing on his lap as if he hadn't had his thigh meat sliced open nearly a week prior.

He groaned as he attempted to roll over and felt the

aching in his leg grow more intense, and immediately he was starting to regret his choice. He had been thinking with his dick instead of his head lately, and it was coming back to bite him in the ass in more ways than one. Haniyf wasn't the only one paying attention to what he had going on. He was moving recklessly and danger always lurked around the corner when you moved with no regard to what was going on around you.

There were rules to the game that he was playing, and he had no clue what he had gotten himself into.

Needing to recover from the sexy fun that he had indulged in while also needing to sleep off the aching in his thigh, it wasn't long before he was drifting back off to sleep.

RAMELLO DIDN'T WAKE up until later that night to the sound of someone tapping quietly on the door and doing their best to call out his name. He jumped down from his cot and went to the door where he found Sierra standing on the other side frantically looking around. It was dark outside. They had been locked down for the night and he was confused as to why she was up there knocking at his door and calling for him.

"Look... be careful when you get up in the morning. Knowledge is suspicious and thinks that we're fuckin'." She whispered to him.

Knowledge was the guy Sierra fucked with in the neighboring dorm whose Facebook page he had gone on to find her for him to find Dominique.

"Okay, just tell him that we not, the fuck?" He was confused. While she had sucked him up with her friend earlier that day, he hadn't stuck his dick in her. What the fuck she had going on with her dude had nothing to do with him.

"He doesn't believe me. He's going to come see you tomorrow and say that you owe him some money for fucking with me. No one's allowed to do that unless they pay his fee." She looked around her, looking for watching eyes, and speaking low in case there were listening ears.

Ramello blinked. *Is this bitch tellin' me that this nigga got her in here sellin' pussy?* He wanted to be shocked, but he wasn't surprised at all. It seemed like it would be some shit that would be in her character to do. If he was about to get caught up, then it was going to be thanks to that hoe-ass bitch. His frustration immediately began to peak.

"Why the hell you just now tellin' me about this shit?" He didn't understand.

He watched her shake her head and step away from the door. "I just came to warn you. Be careful." And before he could say another word, she was walking away and leaving out of the dorm.

"But you ain't fuckin' the nurse, though..." Haniyf said smugly as Ramello got back on his cot, his mind reeling and his thigh throbbing.

"Shut the fuck up..." He wasn't in the mood. Haniyf's deep

chuckle only further frustrated him, but he had no one to blame but himself. He had let pussy blind him and got him moving funny.

At least she put me on point. It would have been ten times worse if that wasn't the case. He then began to wonder if Dominique knew that Sierra sold pussy to the inmates there. The women were complete opposites, that was something that he could tell right away.

Dominique was a reserved and intelligent woman and Sierra seem fun-going and lowkey ratchet. The nurse was hesitant to fuck with him. She had seemed more concerned with losing her license by fucking with him, but her curiosity had gotten the best of her. She had tried to warn him that she couldn't see them being able to make their little rendezvous work out for the long term. Her concerns were legitimate, and it was clear that many more people had picked up on the situation than he would have liked them to, but again he wasn't thinking with the right head.

Ramello was so caught up in his infatuation with the nurse that he completely ignored the basic rules that he had created for himself. He never wanted to be predictable, being predictable meant that people would be able to guess his moves and as he thought back to how he went to the door and had spoken with Sierra every day, and even a couple of times he had disappeared with her. It wasn't a good look at all.

Ramello threw an arm over his eyes and sighed heavily.

He was going to have to do some damage control the next morning.

He pulled his phone out and checked the time. It was just after one in the morning and he decided to shoot Dominique a text. His heart was heavy, he hated that he was going to have to deliver some news that he knew she didn't want to hear. The nurse already had suspected him to be trouble and he had proved exactly that.

In a perfect world everything would have worked out, but because her best friend was a hoe, she had muthafucka's watching her and her every move and it was coming back to bite them both in the ass. Where she thought they were being lowkey, they were anything but thanks to how hot her friend was.

Ramello: Hey... I have some bad news... I think the whole dorm is onto us. Did you know your friend was selling pussy in here? Now she got mufuckas watchin' us and claiming that I owe her nigga some money for fucking with her. Maybe you should take tomorrow off. Just to make sure you're safe until all this shit blows over, you know?

He let out a heavy sigh after he pressed send on the message then let it rest on his belly as he shook his head and took a deep breath. He was going to have to prepare for a fight in case Knowledge was standing on the fact that he owed him money. Ramello wouldn't be paying him for a damn thing. It wasn't his fault that the nigga couldn't control the bitch.

Clearly, she was off fucking on niggas for free and without permission.

The hoe was in violation and was about to bring trouble knocking right on his and Dominique's door. He was convinced so much he felt it in his spirit that shit was about to get sticky, and he wasn't looking forward to it at all.

His main concern wasn't with himself, though. He'd handled Knowledge when he came his way. That too much didn't worry him. What he was worried about was Dominique and what she would think when she realized that their block was hot and hoped like hell that it wouldn't get back to anyone who would fire her.

Only time will tell.

THE FOLLOWING morning Ramello woke up on high alert. After receiving the warning from Sierra the night before, he got up early so he would be up and waiting for the nigga to come pull up on him. One thing he wasn't going to be was a sitting duck for no nigga.

After pulling his phone back out, he checked his messages and saw a message from Dominique.

Dominique: I took the day off... I didn't know that she had all that going on. I knew she was involved with a few inmates, but I didn't know she was doing all of that. She filled me in last night, too...

Dominique: Honestly, I think I may just go ahead and resign, I think that may be the best-case scenario for me. I have to get out of there before shit hits the fan. Things are getting messy.

Ramello's stomach dropped when he read that she was thinking about quitting her job. He felt guilty that he was one of the main contributing factors to her choosing to quit the job.

Ramello: Damn, Nique... I'm sorry. You really think it's necessary to resign? I don't want you to go, and I feel bad that I've contributed to you feeling like you have to do that.

He sighed and sent the message.

Dominique: It's either that or risk them coming for my license. At least if I resign and it comes out once they start investigating, I'll be out of the way and won't be obligated to answer any questions.

Damn... Ramello tiredly ran a hand down his face. He felt bad that what seemed to be a good thing was turning into something sour. He needed to hear her voice, so he called her through the Messenger app again.

"Hello..." Her voice was small as she spoke, she sounded tired.

"Hey... I just needed to hear your voice and know that you were okay." He spoke quietly. Even through the phone, he could pick up on the heavy energy that he knew had to be weighing her down. She could hear it in his voice as well.

"I will be. One way or another I'm going to figure it out. I mean, it's not like I don't have another job working at the hospital. I think it just may be best for me to let the prison job go to preserve my job at the hospital, you know?"

He felt slightly better to know that she had another job so that her financial situation wouldn't be fucked up like he thought it would be. It also intrigued him to know that she had a backup plan. It only confirmed to him that she was a smart woman and it made him like her even more. All the more reason why he was frustrated that he hadn't quite thought through what he had been doing.

Ramello wished like hell that he had thought through the situation more clearly. He felt in his heart that had he done so, what could have come from dealing with Dominique could have been something great. There was no doubt in his mind that she would have been a great asset to the little motion he had going on.

He prayed that he hadn't fucked up a good thing, but it wasn't looking too good.

"I didn't know you worked at a hospital, too. Why do you work here, too, then?" He questioned not wanting to end their conversation yet. It was something that he was curious to know, now. If she worked at a hospital, he was sure that she was paid very well and probably didn't *need* to work at the prison, so he wanted to know how she had ended up there in the first place.

"My dad was in prison my entire life. He got sick one year and the medical staff didn't give him the care that he needed, and he ended up dying... it was the reason that I went to school to become a nurse, and I knew that I always wanted to work in a prison for that exact reason. To make sure that inmates weren't neglected and got the care that they needed."

Her response touched his heart and only made him feel even worse. She had come there on a mission and just like that, he had fucked that up for her. There weren't too many people who worked in the prison system that actually gave a fuck about the inmates there, yet she did, and because of a momentary lack of judgment on both of their behalf's, they had ruined that in less than a week.

He felt like shit.

"That's very kind of you, you know... the fact that you care about the well-being of inmates behind the wall. You don't see that too often around here. You'd be surprised how many of the staff here just sit around and watch niggas die. I hate that things are playing out the way that they are. I low-key regret even pursuing you. I should have left you alone." He rubbed his tired eyes. "I dunno, I just had to have you..."

She let out a soft sigh before she spoke again. "You didn't do anything that I didn't let you. I knew better. Like I said before, there are consequences when it comes to trouble. I got involved and it's backfiring on me. God doesn't allow me to do fuck shit and get away with it." He could hear the pain in her voice and Ramello went quiet.

Dominique was a woman that lived in reality and instead of

blaming Ramello or Sierra for what had happened, she was blaming herself because she could have said no. There was no gun being pointed at her head and yet she still made a conscious choice to fuck with an inmate, knowing that she would be risking her license. She had to hold herself accountable.

She loved working at the prison. It had its days, but for the most part, she found that many of the people who came through her office were decent people who also had lapses in their judgment and had landed behind the wall. In that office, she was reminded that the people in prison were regular people just like her despite some of the crimes some of them had committed.

It took a special kind of person with compassion, patience, and understanding to be able to work in a prison environment and still give the same kind of care that she gave patients in the hospital.

Ramello remembered how gentle and attentive she had been with him while she attended to his wound at that time. Her touch was comforting and unexpectedly soothing, it was one of the main contributors to his dick growing when he was in there. While she was attractive, it was her mannerisms and care that attracted him the most.

"I still feel bad, though."

"Don't," she said softly. "I'll be okay however this all plays out. Everything happens for a reason. This might have just been a sign that it was time for me to quit, anyway. I've been overwhelmed trying to juggle both jobs. It's probably just time for me to let it go."

"I don't want you to leave, though," he admitted.

"I'm sure you don't. If I could have it my way, I'd stay if but if things are as hot as you say... yeah, it may be time for me to go."

"You know what I want, right now?"

He heard her giggle briefly. "What's that, Ramello?"

"Your face in my lap right now." He cracked a grin, reminiscing on the way she gagged on his dick for the first time.

"Of course you do. I know you love this throat. Let's just be happy that we got to experience it. It was good while it lasted, yeah?"

He nodded to himself. "It was damn good. Damn fuckin' good... Aye I got a question... You and yo homegirl... Y'all do that often?"

"You mean me and her?" She laughed at his question.

"Yeah."

"Every once in a while, yeah."

"That's sexy." A goofy grin was on his face.

"Mmhmm... did you enjoy yourself, though? Ever have two women sucking your dick at the same time?"

"Nah, that was a first for me. Shit was fye!" He whistled.

"I'm glad that I was able to give you that. You said it had been seven years, right?" "Yeah, seven long ass years." He sighed heavily at that. He was tired of sitting in prison.

"Well, I'm glad that I was able to give you some... relief."

"For real, though. Thank you for all of that, Nique. A nigga needed that shit. You don't even know, girl."

"Thank *you*. I needed it, too. I work so much, I don't have much time for pleasure and fun in my daily life let alone to date so... you helped me blow off some steam, too. It was good while it lasted."

"You know that won't be the last that we'll see of each other, right?" He needed her to know.

She chuckled. "I'm sure of it. You're quite the persistent one."

"Very." He confirmed with a smirk.

"Right... well, it's been nice chatting with you, Ramello. Since I'm not coming in today, I picked up a shift at the hospital, so I have to start getting ready. You take care, okay?"

"Damn, that sounds like a goodbye." He didn't like the sound of that.

"It is for now, but like you said, we'll see each other again. I don't know when, but one day... until then... you be safe, you hear me? No more gettin' cut up." And there she was being sweet again.

"I ain't gon' make no promises about the last part, but I hear you, shawty. Take care of yourself."

"Goodbye, Ramello."

"Bye, Dominique."

Then the line went dead.

Chapter 7

"You know we got some business to discuss, right?" Knowledge was standing at the door of Ramello and Haniyf's cell, a hard look on his face.

"What business I need to discuss wit' you?" Ramello asked in a bored tone, not bothering to look up from the Cream that he was packing into a finger of a glove.

"Come on, bruh, don't even play me like that. I know you have been in here fuckin' my hoe." Knowledge was a big dude. He stood at about six feet tall and was a fat nigga that waddled around like a penguin. Ramello wasn't intimidated by the man not one bit. In reality, he was cool people, but he wasn't stunnin' that nigga. It would be nothin' for Ramello to mop the floor with his ass.

He stood on his feet and locked eyes with the man. Knowledge had dark circles around his eyes and reminded him of a raccoon. He *definitely* couldn't take that nigga seriously about shit. "Who you talkin' about? I know you ain't talkin' about that bitch out there in the booth... Man, that hoe takes me down to medical. That's it." He stated simply.

"Nah, bruh, niggas already know how this shit go. Niggas don't even talk to my hoe without my permission." Knowledge hit his chest.

"Get the fuck on, bruh. Ain't nobody fuckin' that basic ass bitch." Ramello said, dismissively annoyed.

"You heard my Ahk, bro. Get the fuck on." Haniyf backed up his Muslim brother.

"Aight... aight... I got something for yo ass, watch this." Knowledge nodded his head repeatedly as he walked away from the door.

Ramello shook his head as he resumed packaging up his work. *Hoe ass nigga...* He thought to himself. He didn't know what Knowledge had going on, but he had him fucked up if he thought that he was gonna be moved by all that fake-ass attitude shit. He was deadass wrong, anyway. He wasn't fucking Sierra, shit, Dominique had drained his ass of everything he had before he even got the chance to.

It may have been his only saving grace.

A part of him was curious about how Dominique didn't know what her friend had going on as far as letting Knowledge pimp her out to other inmates, but then again, he could see why. Sierra was reckless. He had heard many stories about the woman fucking and sucking on somebody, but he always assumed that she was just a loose pussy woman, when she was selling it. He didn't know which was worse. Her selling it or giving it out for free.

All he knew was that she wasn't the kind of bitch he would have chosen to fuck with. Even when he did consider it, it was more so out of his need for wanting to fuck her friend, but he was just testing her to see if he *could* fuck her even though she knew that he was involved with her friend. That wasn't the kind of woman he could trust, anyway.

He was shocked as hell when Dominique had her join them during their last session, but the more that he thought about it, it was more so a thing for Dominique rather than him. He enjoyed the experience regardless, though. While he didn't consider it a threesome, he wasn't complaining about having them both sucking his dick and watching Dominique be ravished by her. It was the first time that he had witnessed some girl-on-girl action in person and that was enough for him.

"RAMELLO, bruh, come look at this shit..." Haniyf said looking out the door of their cell and saw Knowledge standing at the door speaking with an LT who had come down to the door unexpectedly.

Right as Ramello walked up to the door, Knowledge turned away from the LT and pointed straight at their cell.

"Naaaw, this bitch ass nigga snitchin'?!" The two men immediately sprang into action, hiding their phones and work. Haniyf had jammed the door, giving them more time to hide their things in case the LT decided that he was going to come up there and fuck with them.

"See, I told yo ass you were hot, but you ain't wanna listen," Haniyf said annoyed that his bunkmate was attracting so much attention to their cell. He didn't want to get caught in the crossfire of the bullshit that he had going on. He was beyond annoyed.

"My bad, man. I fucked up. I'ma make it right, though." He didn't know how but he was going to figure it out.

Fifteen minutes had gone by, and no one had come up to their room. Ramello got up and went to look out the window and saw that the LT had left and hadn't returned. His mind was made up, he had to get Knowledge up outta there.

After allowing another twenty minutes to go by, Ramello pulled his phone out and proceeded to go to Facebook. Clicking on the search button, he searched for Sierra's profile and then sent her a message.

Ramello: You know you fucked up, right? Now yo friend's job is at risk. You gotta fix this shit. How tf you got yo friend out here fuckin' on inmates, encouraging her, yet got her in the dark about what you got goin' on?

Sierra: I know. I know. I just don't know how to fix it. I

didn't think it was going to be a big deal. Knowledge just trippin' right now cause he doesn't trust me.

Ramello: Look... I'ma take care of him. You workin' tonight?

Sierra: Yeah...

Ramello: I'ma let you know when, but I need you to pop that nigga door for me.

Sierra:...

Sierra: You think this will help Mini keep her job? I don't think he said anything yet, but he is saying he'll tell on her because he thinks you're fucking us both. He's been trying to get me to get her to sleep with him for a while now...

That new information pissed him off even more. Now he knew what he was *really* mad about. *Yeah, that nigga up outta here.*

Ramello: Yeah, that nigga won't be a problem no more. I promise you that.

He was going to make sure of it.

Sierra: Just let me know.

Ramello: Let her know not to quit yet and that I'm working on it. Just tell her to use her vacation time for the time being.

Sierra: Okay...

Sierra: Thanks, Ramello.

Ramello: 4sho💯

Not only was he attempting to save himself by getting rid of his problem, but also to help save whatever chance he had at keeping Dominique there with him. He didn't know what it was about her, but he had a good feeling, and he didn't want what they had to end. Not when it was just getting started. They hadn't even scratched the surface of getting to know each other yet.

They weren't going out like that.

With a plan and mind, he got in motion. It was clear that Knowledge was going to be a problem for him from there on out, so the nigga had to go. It was nothing for Ramello to put money on the nigga's head. He knew exactly who he needed to go to and how much it was going to take for him to go handle that business for him.

Ramello made his way to the appropriate cell where he found Eesaa, one of his fellow Muslims who was a lifer. After clearing the room, he got straight to business. "Look, I got an issue with that nigga Knowledge. I got a band for you right now to po' that nigga out and get him up outta here. I got shawty on standby ready to pop his do' tonight."

Eesaa was a tall, light-skinned guy with a bald head, full beard and crazy eye like Fetty Wap. He was known around the Georgia prison system for two things: being a Muslim and steppin' on shit!

He had three consecutive life sentences for slaughtering his baby mama and two of her boyfriends that he found out had all been molesting his daughter. As a result, he had turned into a prison hitman and that's how he made majority of his money. He was comfortable with murder, at times even enjoyed it.

He was sitting on his cot peeling an orange. "Hell, yeah, bruh. Just lemme know when. You still got my app?"

Ramello nodded. "Yup. I'ma letchu know."

"Fasho."

Confident in his plan, Ramello returned to his cell where he sent Eesaa the band and then texted him the screenshot. He called one of his Muslim brothers named, Kwame, who was in the dorm with him and had him pull two junkies in the room. Kwame put them on the phone and Ramello offered them a hundred dollars worth of dope a piece to put Vaseline on end of a dust mop and grease the cameras up when the dorm went to the chow hall. They was with it. Everything was in place. All that was left for him to do now was wait until later that night.

LATER THAT NIGHT AFTER LOCKDOWN, Ramello waited until well into the middle of the night. It was a known fact that Knowledge had a cell to himself. He'd made so much money from Sierra selling pussy for him that he was able to pull strings and get him the cell he preferred with no bunkmate, which was perfect because Eesaa wouldn't have to worry about anyone else being in the room.

Around two in the morning, Sierra slipped into the dorm and checked to see if Knowledge was sleeping before sending Ramello a text from her Apple watch, letting him know that he was dead sleep.

Ramello texted Eesaa to let him know it was time to move and had Sierra pop his door. She watched as Eesaa, who was nothing but a shadow in the dark, calmly walked over to Knowledge's cell on the bottom floor and stood in front of it, then popped the lock. Swiftly, he disappeared into the room and less than a minute later he was exiting the room and made his way back into his.

Ramello's phone buzzed in his hand. It was a text message of a thumbs-up emoji and a smirked tugged at one corner of his lips.

It was quick, quiet, and went down without a hitch.

Bitch ass nigga, Ramello's last thought. *All that cap.*

He put his phone away before he peacefully went to sleep, dreaming of when he would get to see Dominique again.

THE NEXT MORNING WAS CHAOS. Knowledge was found laying dead in his cot with his throat slit, during morning count time. The Warden called an Emergency count and locked the whole compound down. After the body had been removed from the cell, everyone was shaken down and remained on lockdown for another two weeks.

They had never figured out who had slaughtered the man, and it wouldn't make much of a difference if they had. Ramello had handled his business, freed Sierra from the toxic and abusive relationship that she had with Knowledge, and eliminated the threat to Dominique, her job, and their budding relationship.

DOMINIQUE: I can't wait to see you, today.

Ramello smiled at the text that he woke up to from his little freaky nurse. She was returning to work and had every intention of linking up with him and thanking him for what he had done for her and her friend.

Ramello: I can't wait to see you either ;)

After taking a shower and getting himself presentable for his woman, he made his way to the front door, dramatically limping to make it seem like he needed to go to medical where a new officer sat at the booth.

"'Scuse me, ma'am. I need to go to medical. I think my leg is infected." He lied. Already had been prepared, he had taken a couple of ketchup packets and spread it on his pants to make it look like he had a blood stain.

The white woman sitting at the booth looked at him with wide eyes rushed to let him through the door and began rushing him to the back. "Oh my God! Are you okay?! Let's get you to the nurse." She offered him a hand and then helped him limp to the medical office.

After the whole fiasco with Knowledge, as soon as the job had been done, Sierra quit. No longer did she feel comfortable being there knowing that so many people had dirt hanging over her head and others were trying to recruit her into being their hoe. She decided that being a Correctional Officer wasn't for her. At only thirty, she still had time to pivot and find a career more suitable for her.

He had to bite back a smile as soon as Dominique opened the door and he met her eyes. He pursed his lips to keep from laughing when she pretended to be in shock at the "blood" seeping through his pants.

"Oh! Come on, hun, let's get you cleaned up." She said and looked at the white woman. "Thank you, Chelsea. I got it from here."

She nodded and closed the door behind her.

As soon as the door closed, Ramello bit into his lip and grabbed his dick through his pants as he watched Dominique turn around and lock the door. Approaching her from behind he pressed his hard dick against her back.

Her heartbeat wildly in her chest, and her clit throbbed with desire. She was breathing heavily, unable to hide how turned on she was to be so close to him again when he slid her bottoms down her legs. She felt heat against her.

"I miss you touching me." She said when she felt his rough hands on her inner thighs, caressing her soft flesh.

Ramello grabbed her by one of her wide bare hips and slid the other hand farther up between her thighs and allowed two of his fingers to slide between her pussy lips, groaning at how wet she was. He had barely touched her, and she was already ready to take his dick.

Dominique moaned when he began planting wet kisses along her neck and shoulders. Her thick body melted into his as he caressed her body and toyed with her wet pussy with his fingers.

"Mmm, fuck, mama, this pussy is so fuckin' juicy." He rasped in her ear, sinking a thick finger into her tight pussy. He loved the way that it clenched tightly around his index as he stroked it in and out of her. His dick throbbed painfully in his pants; he wanted her so badly. But he wanted to savor his time with her. He didn't want to rush it.

Dominique couldn't help but moan in response to his words and the way that he fucked her pussy with his finger. She had been longing for him for weeks. "Oh, baby…" She moaned, pushing her ass back against him, wanting his finger to fuck her deeper.

"Bend that this phat ass over, mama. Let me give this pretty pussy what it needs." He murmured in her ear. Removing his finger from her moist cave, he slapped her ass.

She whimpered with delight at the sting on her ass from the slap, slid her scrubs down, and did as he said. Ramello pulled her back up to lift her shirt over her head, and her Double-D's bounced out in the prettiest cream lace bra he'd ever seen. Moving in sync, they made their way to the medical table where she steadied her juicy body on her hands and knees and waited in anticipation for what he was about to do to her next.

"Ahhh!" She moaned and dropped her face into the table when she felt Ramello's thick, wet tongue snaking up the folds of her pussy and flicking firmly across her clit. "Oh, yes, baby!"

"Mmmmmm." He moaned as he lapped at her pussy, using his long tongue to fuck her tight, pink pussy hole. The taste of her pussy drove him wild with lust yet again.

"Fuck, yeah. Oh, you eatin' me so fuckin' good, right now. I needed this, baby." Dominique's eyes rolled in the back of her head as she started to throw her ass back against his face, making his tongue fuck her pussy even deeper.

Removing his tongue from her creamy hole, he licked his way down to her clit where he trapped it between his thick lips. Dominique moaned loudly and threw her ass back faster, loving the sensation of her clit being tugged and sucked on.

"Oh my God! Don't stop, baby! Don't stop! You 'bout to make this pussy cum!" She cried breathlessly as he brought her closer and closer to a desperately needed orgasm.

She reached a hand between her legs and cupped Ramello's face, holding it in place as she fucked his mouth. "Yes! Yes! Yes! Yes!" She said in strangled moans, struggling to keep quiet, her entire body trembled as she neared her peak. "Ah—" She screamed, and moaned uncontrollably, toppling forward as her orgasm hit her hard and deliciously, sending her into euphoria.

Ramello got up from his kneeled position on the floor and smirked down at the trembling nurse, loving the way her rolls rippled and bounced with her every movement. He stripped out of his clothes, his hard dick springing up, long and strong when he removed his pants and stepped out of them.

Dominique was still on her face, attempting to catch her breath and recover from the most intense orgasm that she had ever had in her life, when he grabbed her by her thighs and flipped her over and onto her back, making her look up at him with wide eyes. She was surprised that he had been able to flip her so easily, but it only made her pussy pulse and drip for him even more.

"I have been wanting to get back in this pussy for so fuckin' long..." He said as he got up onto the bed and spread Dominique's legs wide so that he could get a full view of her wet pussy.

Dominique laid on her back, horny and needy as she went back and forth with herself about how wrong it was to be fucking this inmate, but she couldn't get enough of him. It was so *wrong* but felt so fuckin' *right*. She couldn't deny herself the opportunity to feel his big, black dick stroking her pussy to ecstasy.

Grabbing her ankles, she held her thighs back and spread them wide, exposing her pussy to him. It was ready, wet, creaming, and screaming for him to fuck her. She looked up at him with needy eyes, whimpering as he slapped her clit repeatedly with his dick and teased her hole by slipping the head in and out of her, and running it slowly up and down her glistening slit.

He finally sunk his dick deep into her, pushing himself into her until her fat pussy swallowed every inch of his length. "Goddamn, you so fuckin' tight and wet."

"Ssssss! Mmmmm…" Dominique moaned, gripping her ankles tighter, and spreading her thighs wider as he stroked in and out of her pussy steadily. His thick dick stretched her tight pussy wide.

"Fuck, yo pussy is so fuckin' juicy and creamy. I love that shit." Ramello said in awe, watching his dick slip in and out of her, loving the way that it coated his dick in her juices and cream.

Dominique laid back and closed her eyes as she welcomed the pleasure of feeling a dick inside of her once again. The fact that it was an inmate she knew she shouldn't have been fucking while she was on the clock stroking her to another fast-approaching orgasm only made it that much more erotic and pleasurable for her. "Mmmm! Fuck me harder, baby!" She begged him.

He did as she asked and began pounding into her pussy, laying on top of her and kissing her deeply, slipping his tongue in her mouth and engaging in a battle with hers as he stroked in and out of her juicy box roughly. Ramello loved the feeling of her pussy gushing around his dick and dripping down his balls, making her wet up the table beneath them.

"Oooooh, I'm cummin', baby! I'm—" She snatched her mouth away from his and he had to clamp a hand over her mouth to keep her quiet while her pussy spasmed around his dick.

He groaned in her ear as he stroked wilding in and out of her, unable to get enough of how good her pussy felt wrapped around his dick as she came on it. She was so fuckin' hot and felt like home to him, he didn't ever wanna stop fucking her.

Dominique felt his dick swelling deep inside of her and knew that he was close. "Mhm, yeah, baby. I'ma cum all in this pussy."

"Yeah, Daddy, cum in me." She encouraged him, reaching a hand between them and rubbing her fat clit. "I wanna feel your hot cum filling my pussy up," she said with a whimper, looking him in his eyes and using her free hand to pinch and roll one of her nipples. She was so fuckin' horny and she never wanted him to stop fucking her.

She couldn't believe how good he was making her feel. She cried. Tears of joy, pleasure, and appreciation dripped down her face. She loved every minute of it.

"Shit, I'm 'bout to buss all in this good ass pussy," he groaned, grabbing her hands and pinning them to the bed above her head and pounding her pussy roughly.

"Uggh," Ramello cried loudly as he stroked one last time and exploded deep inside the nurse's pussy, spurt after spurt of cum slashing hard against the walls of Dominique's insides, filling her up to the very brink. After, he collapsed on top of her, hugging her body tightly as he experienced the aftershocks of his orgasm. She was soft, thick, and smelled good. Dominque cupped his face in her hands and pulled his lips to meet hers in a passionate kiss.

"Who would have fuckin' thought... A nurse and her favorite inmate," Dominique said with a giggle when they pulled away from the kiss.

Ramello smirked down at her; his dick still buried inside of her. "And now you stuck wit' me, shawty. We locked in forever now."

The End

Did you enjoy the read?
Let us know how much by leaving us a review on Amazon
and Goodreads.

. . .

Keep reading for a preview of…

The Hottest Summer Ever

By Elijah R. Freeman

PROLOGUE

eluctant

LIGHTING FLASHED, thunder boomed and heavy rain pelted the top of the stolen Toyota Corolla as I made my way home. Feeling like time was working against me, I pushed the car past the speed limit, throwing caution to the wind. I was in a lot of pain. The adrenaline rush from my mission had subsided and the wear and tear on my shoulder was catching up to me. There was no time to acknowledge pain though. More imperative issues were on my mind. Like why Keisha hadn't told us about the unexpected visit that caused her not to eradicate all traces left by the crew. We could have done damage control before things had gotten this far.

Everyone was dead now. No wonder Keisha had backed

out of the streets to go legit. She was running from her past. Her karma. Yet it found her. Her, Redd and Polo; and there was still a loose end unattended. A loose end with all the answers to my remaining questions but would create new problems. Seeing who I'd just seen moments ago reminded me just how small the world really was. It also reiterated the fact that anything was possible and to always expect the unexpected. That along with my knowledge of Zoepound and the little I remember of what Keisha disclosed about them confirmed my suspicions and broke my heart at the same time. Redd was right.

I pulled into the driveway and sat there, trying to fix myself up in an attempt to stop the pain, physical and emotional. It was 4 am. I didn't want to do it but I grabbed my strap. My life was damaged beyond repair. Chelsea was the single thread that held it together. Without her, my whole world would fall apart. What was the point in having money if there was no one to share it with? No one from the bottom to look back with from the top. I'd spend the rest of my life in question. Wondering if the people around me loved me for me, or simply for what I could do for them. That's no way for a woman to live. A lot could've been different, and staring at the gun in my hands, all the mistakes I made throughout life came rushing back...

CHAPTER 1

CRUSHED DREAMS

Born and raised in College Park, it's no surprise that I turned out to be a product of my environment. I was born to Richard and Nicole Love on March 28th, 1990 at Grady Memorial, one of Georgia's prominent hospitals. At the last minute before signing my birth certificate they decided on a name, Richelle Kemoni Love. Then a few days after I was pronounced healthy, my mother was discharged and they were finally able to take me home to our small apartment on Godby Road.

I was daddy's little girl. Whatever I wanted, I got. I loved my mama, but me and daddy just always had a deeper relationship. Daddy felt children were smarter than what a lot of people gave them credit for. As a result, he spoke to me as if I was a lot older than I actually was. I was always with him, even when he would stop by some of his stash houses. He never sheltered me from what was going on, and because of this, I grew up more advanced than most kids in my neighborhood. For me, there was no Santa Clause, Easter bunny or Prince Charming. It was just daddy, my knight in shining armor. He was my everything. His every movement was geared towards providing for me and mama, and to give me the life he never had. For a while he did. My daddy, my uncle Ron, and their childhood friend, Big Rod had found a plug and was on the come up. Then one night everything changed.

I was nine when my daddy was killed. He was just starting to make a name for himself in the dope trade. The competition felt the need to get rid of him. It was the summer of '99. I was awakened from my sleep by a loud commotion. Daddy always told me never to come looking if I sensed trouble in the house. I didn't. I went to hide instead, lying flat on my back in the bathtub. Moments later there were gunshots. I closed my eyes and prayed to the heavens.

It was another thirty minutes before I left the tub and tip-toed down the stairs, peeking around corners. Whoever it had been was long gone. I made my way over to the living room, tears came streaming from my eyes. I was young but I lived in the hood and was no stranger to gunshot wounds. I picked up the phone, dialed 911, and told them my daddy had been shot. I ran over to see if he was okay. I was crying profusely. I could barely see when I knelt down beside him. "Never forget everything I taught you." Those were his last words.

"I love you, daddy. Don't leave me."

He smiled... and that was that.

When mama and the police finally arrived, daddy was long gone. Responses to calls for help from Godby were always slow.

Daddy never kept work in the house, but he was a known drug dealer. The authorities wrote his death off as drug-related. They didn't care. He was just one less nigga they had to worry about. Mama and I moved into an apartment in Red Oak Projects that daddy had in case of an emergency. Big Rod would check up on us from time to time, but my uncle disappeared. No one told me where he went, and when I asked, they acted like it was a secret or something. Big Rod took me to get ice cream often after my daddy died. Every Friday I would wait anxiously in the window for him to show up in his money green El Dorado. He would get out standing tall, big and black, putting you in the mind of Bruce-Bruce. I was always happy to see him and ran out the door to greet him, jumping up and down knowing that I was about to receive something to my childish delight. Mama liked it, too. It gave her a break.

Big Rod would lift me up, spin me around and put me in the front seat. It was on one of these days while waiting in line for ice cream at a Dairy Queens in Riverdale that some tall, bald, dark skin guy wearing blue jeans, all white soulja Reebox and a Lakers Jersey approached Big Rod and asked about my uncle.

"Heard anything from ya boy Ron?"

Big Rod shook his head. "No, and you won't either. Nobody has. I'm starting to think he's dead."

"That would be best for him," the man scoffed. He started to walk off but noticed me, and paused.

I turned to look up at Big Rod, who stared back at the man expressionless. I looked back at the man, he looked up at Big Rod and shook his head.

"That's crazy," he said.

Without another word, he walked away. Five minutes later, we got our ice cream, left, and headed to Riverdale Park where Big Rod watched me play until the sun began to set.

Weeks turned into months and as the year went on, ice cream Fridays with Big Rod became less frequent, and before I knew it, he stopped showing up altogether. That's when things changed and I began to feel the weight of my reality.

Mama was one of the baddest bitches in the hood until she started fucking with that shit. And yes, I do mean crack. She had a bitch ass boyfriend named Darrel who was always watching me. At ten years old, I was ignorant of the lust in his eyes and he eventually violated me. I had just come home from school and mama wasn't there, so that bastard had his way with me. She must have been chasing the best high of her life because she didn't return for hours.

Darrel was sitting on the sofa watching *Leprechaun In The Hood* when he saw me. "Hey baby."

"What the fuck? I'm not your baby," I said.

I went to my room to change clothes. I could feel the vibe of someone watching me. I turned around to find it was Darrel's nasty ass. These mere events along with the fact that he used to beat my mama were the reasons I was filled with distaste and rage when it came to him. "Get away from my door!" I yelled.

He came in, closing the door behind him. "Making big demands for someone so little."

He reached for me. I tried to run but he slapped the shit out of me. The force from his strong hand sent me reeling to the floor. I was disoriented and seeing stars as he began removing the rest of my clothes. "Just take it and the pain will go away," he spoke through clenched teeth. I was scared and tears were abundantly rolling down my cheeks. "I've been wanting this for a long time," he said, pinning me down with a rough grunt.

I tried to fight back but he was stronger than me. Every time I tried to buck on him taking off my clothes he would slap me. Eventually, he got me naked and jammed his dick inside me. He broke my hymen and tore my insides apart. It hurt so bad. I cried and screamed the whole time. Blood was everywhere.

There are some things you can't see happening to you until they do. That was the day I stopped believing in God. I was only in the fifth grade and he'd done nothing but make my life hell. I figured I couldn't be sent to hell if I was already there. I didn't tell mama. She was too *dickmitized*. Plus, he was the one bringing in what little food we did have, if that counts for anything. Thursdays and Fridays were his days off and he wanted me to be there. On the days I wasn't, he would beat me. This went on for a while until I was more than fed up with his shit.

I awoke to him arguing with mama one morning. It escalated and I came to her defense. "Get off my mama!" I was trying to pull him away from her. I never saw his hand. I felt it, it sent me flying to the wall. My mouth was bleeding and my ears were ringing.

"Leave my baby alone!" my mama screamed from the floor of our small living room.

He stomped her and told her to shut up. That's when I ran out of the living room and came back with Darrel's .38 special. With hot, angry tears pouring down my face, I screamed at the top of my lungs for him to get off my mama. He turned and looked me in the eyes.

"Shoot me, bitch, if you got the heart."

I thought about all the shit he did to me, and I pulled the trigger twice.

BWA! BWA!

His eyes were a mixture of shock and disbelief as he hit the floor, bleeding to death. The gun fell from my trembling hands. Mama screamed like Tyra Banks in *Higher Learning*. I sat on the carpet and stared at Darrel's lifeless body. The nosy ass neighbors called the police and they took me away. I did ten months in the Metro RYDC.

Mama never came to see me, let alone claim me and I was eventually placed in a group home in the middle of Hillandale, another neighborhood in College Park with seven other girls. All of them were lame as hell, except one. Her name was Chelsea. I didn't know much about her because she never talked about her past. Still and yet, for some reason, I liked her in the type of way I should've liked boys. A lot of girls hated me because all the boys wanted me, but I wasn't even interested in them, to be honest. I was attracted to pretty girls. I dressed feminine but I had more nigga tendencies than the average girl should. I guess because of the way I grew up. At least that's what I came to believe.

Everybody had a mentor who brought them things, except me, and when they came to visit the group home, I'd be assed out every trip. For months, I used to cry myself to sleep until one day I decided something had to shake. Now in the seventh grade, niggas would try to fuck with me but I would never buy into it. I knew what niggas wanted, and it didn't turn me on. I was repulsed by the thought of a dick inside of me. Chelsea turned me on, though. We were basically joined at the hip. She turned out to be quite gorgeous. She was a redbone with a petite frame, cute face, like one of those Disney girls, with long brown hair to frame it.

Anyway, when I realized I didn't like boys, I tended to keep a lot of female company. To my surprise niggas started to hate on me, throwing salt on my name when they could. All but one, his name was Redd. He had a light brown skin tone. His dreads were to his neck and he stood about five-nine with a medium build. His grandparents were strong believers in the teachings of Marcus Garvey, and his parents were Rootical Rastafarians who believed in the holistic way of life. While they were full Jamaicans who came to the States in the '80s, Redd grew up on Gresham Road in East Atlanta. He was a Grady baby to the fullest.

His family had come to America on a banana boat, running from the Kingston authorities. Once here, they changed their last name to Hicks and started over. Arriving in the middle of the crack era, Redd's father, Jamaica Ray, learned the recipe and went to work. He put together a crew of thoroughbreds and painted the city red. At the height of his success with Jamaican novelty shops, a Caribbean Cuisine spot, and a club called Amadu's, Raphael Hicks was born. That was two years before my time.

By Redd's eleventh birthday so much attention had been drawn to Jamaica Ray. The Feds had an ongoing investigation and eventually seized everything he owned. Jamaica Ray was arrested and extradited to Jamaica where he would never see the light of day again. Redd's mother was taken into Federal custody for several murders, conspiracy, and drug trafficking charges. Guilty with no way to escape, the woman hung herself. She was found in her cell one morning during breakfast. Redd said she was believed to have been pregnant, but he wasn't sure. It was sad.

Subsequently, Redd was adopted by a money hungry couple who didn't care how long he stayed out, what he did or who he did it with. Redd lived a lawless life. He believed that, because he was from ATL, he was above the law. He didn't take shit from nobody and his reputation made a lot of people scared of him.

Redd and I started rocking with each other. We smoked so much damn weed he started calling me Kush, and the name stuck. My girlfriends would get mad because they thought I was fucking him, but that wasn't the case. We were just cool. We even had our own secret duck off, that only we knew about, down the street from Mary McLeod Bethune Elementary. We'd meet there whenever Redd had stolen something and wanted to show off, which was often.

My first lick was with him. I was pretty fucking nervous. Not because it was my first, but because it was a dope boy named Champ. He had pull all through the city. At the age of eighteen, he had more money than most niggas his age. I mean, he wasn't Big Meech or nothing but he damn sure was plugged in. Redd didn't seem to care, so I said fuck the shit too. His spot was on the eastside and I hardly went out that way.

We went in through the window of his ground level home in Meadow Lane off Glenwood Road. We found a .380, eight hundred dollars, and some weed. Redd said it was a Quarter Pound.

Although we didn't get much, Redd let me keep the .380. That was my first strap. The money and weed were split down the middle. Four hundred was the most I ever had in my pocket. Most of my money came from females I fucked with. I had a mouthpiece for a bitch because I knew what they wanted. Chelsea would get mad when she saw me with other girls. Couldn't say I blamed her, though. I was jealous at times myself. The only difference was I never showed it. I had a reputation to keep. I could have any bitch I wanted and the ones who got no talk were green with envy.

I was jumped more times than I care to remember. I stayed getting into fights and stayed thirsty to hit licks with Redd. He just seemed to know so much. I began to see him as my only way out the hood but he saw hitting licks as his only way out. Still, we were all we had.

Available Now

BOOKS BY

URBAN AINT DEAD's C.E.O

<u>Elijah R. Freeman</u>

Triggadale

Triggadale 2

Triggadale 3

Tales 4rm Da Dale

The Hottest Summer Ever

Murda Was The Case

Murda Was The Case 2

Murda Was The Case 3

Hittin' Licks For The Holidays: Atlanta

OTHER BOOKS BY

URBAN AINT DEAD

Tales 4rm Da Dale

The Hottest Summer Ever

Hittin' Licks For The Holidays: Atlanta

By **Elijah R. Freeman**

Despite The Odds

By **Juhnell Morgan**

Good Girl Gone Rogue

By **Manny Black**

Hittaz

Hittaz 2

Hittaz 3

Hittaz 4

Coldhearted

By **Lou Garden Price, Sr.**

Charge It To The Game

Charge It To The Game 2

A Summer To Remember With My Hitta

Snatched Up By A Hitta

Santa Sent Me A Real One For Christmas

Wet Dreams on Lockdown: The Unit Manager

By **Nai**

A Setup For Revenge

By **Ashley Williams**

Ridin' For You

Trickin' on a Heaux for Christmas: A BBW Love Story

Homie Hoppin' For The Holidays

By **Telia Teanna**

The State's Witness

The State's Witness 2

The State's Witness 3

By **Kyiris Ashley**

Stuck In The Trenches

Stuck In The Trenches 2

By **Huff Tha Great**

The Swipe

By **Toōla**

Melted the Heart of a Menace

By P. Wise

Merry Trapmas: Ice & Frost

By **Mia Sky**

Thug Me The Right Way

By **DiamondATL & Nai**

Ridin For You, Too
Wet Dreams On Lockdown: The Female C.O
By **Telia Teanna**

A Setup For Revenge 2
Wet Dreams On Lockdown: The Librarian
By **Ashley Williams**

A Gangsta's Last Kiss
By **Mia Sky**

Pretti & The Beast
Wet Dreams On Lockdown: Lieutenant Grace
By **P. Wise**

Wet Dreams On Lockdown: The Counselor
By **Paris Iman**

Wet Dreams On Lockdown: The Male C.O
By **Tamyra Griffin**

Wet Dreams On Lockdown: The Captain
By **TN Jones**

Wet Dreams On Lockdown: The Warden
By **Shawnice**